LOST RIVER

by Roger Sheffer

NIGHT TREE PRESS
Boonville, New York

The stories "Amazing Grace" and "Heat and Hot Water" appeared
in their original form in the Adirondack literary magazine *Blueline.*
Many thanks to *Blueline* and its editor, Alice Gilborn, for allowing
these stories to appear in this collection in revised form.

Cover by Randy Justice
Book design by Nancy Doss
Text set in Paladium by The Right Type, Shepherdstown, WV

Published by
NIGHT TREE PRESS
Gregg Fedchak, Publisher
R.D.#2, Box 140-G
The Gorge Road Rt. 46
Boonville, New York 13309

Library of Congress Catalog Number 88-90528
ISBN 0-935939-02-4

"He sat on a log, the invisible compass in his hand, while the secret night-sounds which had ceased at his movements scurried again and then fell still for good and the owls ceased and gave over to the waking day birds and there was light in the gray wet woods and he could see the compass."

—Faulkner, *The Bear*

PREFACE

Lost River refers not only to the last story in this collection and the frozen river that runs through it, but also to the small, fictional Adirondack township in which most of these stories take place. It is a thinly populated town—with fewer than a hundred year-round residents (perhaps five hundred more in summer) and no real business district. The isolated gas stations, bars, and general stores occur almost at random, never in any coherent pattern.

To see a doctor or make a bank deposit, the people must drive twenty miles south to Williston or Tannersburgh (fictional Adirondack border towns); to see a stockbroker, they drive to Utica or Schenectady. But the typical Lost River residents do none of the above. They hang out at the bars and general stores or stay home all day, particularly in January or February, when they approach total paralysis of body and spirit.

Unlike the more celebrated parts of the Adirondack Park, Lost River is not scenic. From the highway there are occasional views of lakes, but few mountain vistas, the best being from the south shore of Silver Lake where the expensive camps are located, on a road with a sign that warns, "Private—No Thoroughfare." The year-round residents are only vaguely aware of the mountain-tops, the subtle charms enjoyed by the seasonal visitor. Lost River people rarely look up anyway. They tend to have a truncated vision of their town— they know the roads, they know the snowmobile trails that lead to their favorite bars, they've seen (though they wish they hadn't) the pernicious rot that eats away at the foundation of their modest homes. This becomes ironic for the handyman (the most honorable local profession) who labors all winter to maintain the rich people's summer palaces when his own home is a trailer or a shack.

Lost River is a part of the Adirondacks where you can walk a marked trail all day in the middle of July and never meet another human being. You can ski all day, but you'll have to break your own trail. The businessmen always speculated that the hikers and skiers would come, but they never did.

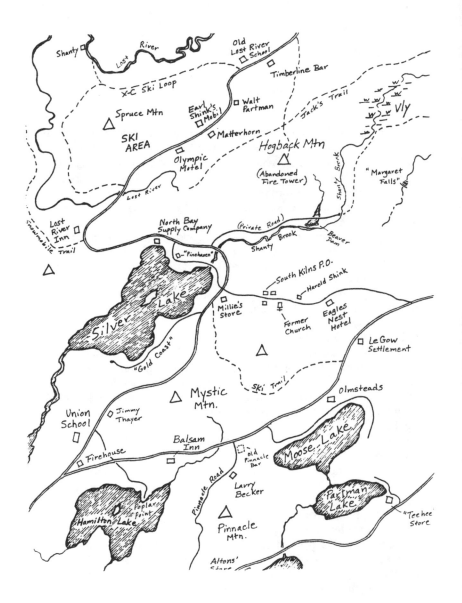

TABLE OF CONTENTS

DEER FLIES

When I awake in the middle of the night, I can tell where I am without the aid of light or sound, by touching the fresh insect bites around my ankles, a ring of bumps marking where my socks end. It's those Silver Lake deer flies—you wear a hat to keep them off your head and they go right for the ankles.

In the city, a car passing my house will light up the window, but out here the lights from the highway cannot penetrate the thick hemlocks, and only the quivering sound of tires washes through the woods, not the actual sound of the tires but a ghostly echo sifting through, almost breaking apart into the sound of night-insects before it reaches my cabin. All my windows are open, the screens mended and back in place.

Twice a day I ride my bicycle to Millie's general store at East Bay, only a half mile from here, most of the way on an oiled dirt road that parallels the state highway (and used to *be* the state highway), keeping one hand on the handlebar and the other circling in the air to fend off the deer flies that hover about my head but seldom land. Once in a while a deer fly gets in my ear and sputters a complaint, and I wonder why natural selection hasn't weeded out the noisier members of the species, to create a quieter insect, one that will go about its blood-sucking work in silence and dignity.

I make a trip to the store both mornings and afternoons because the ice box is small—and there's not much to do at the cabin except read; no guests this week and not much dish washing. The Schenectady Gazette comes in with the mail at ten, and I stand patiently on the covered porch, avoiding the three places where the rain drips through fist-sized holes, while Millie separates the reserved papers from the ones she'll put out on the rack. I listen to her mutter as she checks the names on her list: "Oh, she's not here

yet, she can't *stand* the flies . . . and he *may* or he may *not* be, but
if he is, and he don't get his paper, he'll never let me hear the end of
it, and I got better things to do than to listen to that old fool crab
about his paper . . . I don't make a dollar a day on these darned
papers, they oughta know that. My labor's worth five cents an
hour at this rate . . ."

She has a sign on the peanut barrel inside—"My yearly profet.
Go ahead, take a few," consistent with other misspelled signs
around the store, "You brake it, you've bougth it," and the like.
She tells me she used to teach school, but that was a long time ago,
when they *had* a school up here. Over seventy, with a high
forehead, long nose, and an age spot large enough and in the right
position to be mistaken at a distance for a third eye, Millie's face
serves as sufficient warning to all who might consider misbehaving
in her store.

While I wait on the porch, I often take a peek at the Enquirer or
the Weekly World News. I never buy those papers; the one time I
put the Weekly World News on the counter ("Siamese Twins
Switch Husbands") Millie refused to ring it up. "I'm sorry, Mr. Bob
Carpenter, but that's not the kind of paper I'd ever write *your* name
on," she told me as she stashed it in her reserve box. "I'm gonna
save this one for Harold. He was asking about it, wondering when
it came in. And this is the only one they sent up this time."

Harold Shink lives at Silver Lake all year, but not on the lake. He's
the caretaker for most of the summer camps on the north shore from
Shanty Brook Inlet to Bluff Point, after which the shore is mostly
State-owned until you get to the Gold Coast along the south shore.
Harold takes care of two or three fancy camps on the Gold Coast.

You can't drink the water from the lake.

So every June first, Harold has several five-gallon jugs of spring
water lined up on my back porch, and a note: "For your coffee and
orange juice, and boiling sweet corn, and brushing your teeth and
you name it. Refills in two weeks, or sooner by request." Every
word is spelled correctly. The wooden float he built for me last
September is twenty feet out from the shore, anchored exactly the
way I want it. And the roof is still in place; it hasn't collapsed
during the winter, because Harold has gone up there with his long-
handled rake after every big storm.

We are forty miles from the nearest bank, so I pay Harold by depositing a three-hundred dollar check at the store the day I arrive for the summer—more than that if he's done special jobs for me— and from this he draws a large part of his subsistence. I've stood behind him in line at the store often enough to know that his subsistence never varies much: there's the six-pack of Genny Creme Ale in bottles; the one pound of orange American cheese, sliced a quarter inch thick (he calls it Velveeta, but I think it's generic orange cheese); the small can of Vienna sausages; the long loaf of Sunbeam white bread; two or three boxes of chocolate chip cookies; and the dirty magazines and tabloids Millie reserves for him. Often, Millie's prepared everything in advance and has his order in a box. "That way," she confided, "I don't have to talk to him."

Sometimes there's five gallons of kerosene she lets him pump for himself from the old blue tank by the side of the store, although the sign says, "No self-service." The first time I met Harold, it wasn't exactly face to face; he was bent over at the blue kerosene tank, his pants falling down, half of his rear end exposed.

I believe I'm the only person who talks to him, beyond the elementary this-and-that dialogue he has with Millie in the store when the order isn't quite to his liking—"Could you check to see if you put all the magazines out there," or "I'm wondering whether you got any more of that olive loaf," or "Go easy on the Velveeta this time; how much of a balance do I got left in there—five dollars?"

My porch roof leaks. The other day we had two inches of rain, and a half inch of that rain leaked through onto the back porch where I pile up my old copies of the Gazette, and where I like to sit in the red rocker with the rush seat when it's raining and the power's out, and I need the best possible light to read the small print.

I get on my bike and head for the store. The deer flies haven't come out from where they've hidden during the rain, but puddles have formed where I assume future generations may breed and then buzz out to thrive on the blood from my scalp and ankles. The stream that runs only when it rains more than an inch is trying to cut a channel across the road.

I need to get in touch with Harold, but Harold doesn't have a phone at his place and makes me leave all my messages with Millie. True, Millie has a phone, so I guess I've turned this leaking roof into another excuse to go down to the store and peek at the dirty magazines and crazy tabloids.

She gives me a look with her third eye and says, "You again!" and then goes on with her vigorous sweeping.

"I have a message for Harold."

"Well, I'll tell ya," she says, tossing the broom into the alcove that used to be the East Bay post office. "It won't do you no good to leave it with me at the store, as Harold's been making himself scarce around here the last few days."

"But do you know where he is?"

She says, "Sure, I can tell you exactly where he's at. Not that I'm the nosy type, but Harold does have his rainy-day activities." She smiles, then puckers her lips to push the loose dentures back in place.

"Then I don't want to intrude on anything," I say. "Did the latest *People* come in?"

"Tomorrow with the mail," she says quickly. "Intrude on anything? Ha! Well, it wouldn't be that much, if you know Harold. The only people talk to him are his father and his sister, and them only because Harold puts the food on the table, such as it is. 'Pass the Velveeta, Harold'—that sort of thing." Then she smiles as if to say she didn't mean to disparage the food, since it came from her store.

She pounds her fist on Harold's account book, a three-by-five tablet in which various memos and receipts have been folded.

"To wrap it up in one simple sentence, Harold Shink is a fat and disgusting thing for me to look at every day." Sounds as if she's wrapped up a bad cut of meat in some of her deli paper—which has been known to occur. "But it wasn't always the case," she continues, almost sorry she has spoken unkindly of him. "Nope. When I taught the fourth and fifth grade up in the old Lost River School—it's on State land now, you know, so they tore the building down—anyway, back in those days I remember Harold was a darling, beautiful, smart boy and dear to my heart. Things changed an awful lot in thirty years."

It's hard to imagine Harold as a beautiful boy. I've owned a camp on Silver Lake only five years, and all I know is the present version: a bald man with a bushy overhanging mustache and an overhanging beer belly. It would be easy to draw a caricature. In warm weather, he wears a green plaid flannel shirt with the sleeves cut high enough to show off a Navy tattoo—the torso and head of a blond woman—on his muscular upper arm. His nails are dirty and warped from too many misses with the hammer. He picks his nose with what's left of his nails. But I've seen worse in this town.

Millie tops off the Salem column of the cigarette rack. "You'd cry to see the picture of him as a young boy. I got one upstairs in the living room, with my Lost River kids all lined up in two rows out in front of the schoolhouse. I bet you couldn't pick him out. Margaret's not in the picture. You wanna know why?"

"Not really. Millie, I've got important work for Harold. Help me find him." If I let her go on about her school kids, there's no telling what might happen.

"Go down to the Eagles Nest Hotel," she says, pointing that way. "Since they put in some kind of satellite, he's been watching the Playboy Channel at all hours when he ought to be working on his camps. You see him, Bob, you tell him I got a half-dozen messages folded into his account book. It's gettin' too fat to stick back in the slot." She demonstrates this for me. The book hangs out obscenely.

"Okay."

"And you tell him he's only got a fifty-dollar balance. Keep him in his Velveeta for a week, and then—pffft." She makes the gesture of a punctured balloon—as if that is what would happen to Harold when the Velveeta ran out.

The road to the Eagles Nest winds away from the lake, semi-paved and hard on the bike, over a high meadow lined by wild sweet pea and yellow cinquefoil, and down into a dogpatch community where most of the residents are probably related even if they're not talking to each other.

I've never ridden my bicycle through here before, never slowed down and paid attention to the way the locals live in South Kilns—the odd name of this hamlet. South Kilns has a log-cabin post office, next to a snowmobile dealer in a low white metal building, crumpled badly on one side and held together with duct tape. Then a building that must have been a church at one time, boarded up now, with a steeple that looks as if it was pinched by giant fingers. And then a couple of real houses, featuring ceramic deer and waterfowl; but mostly mobile homes, some partially encased in wood structures—as if they might eventually be swallowed up. Many have extensive lawns, some well-kept, where they offer perpetual yard sales, or announce on hand-lettered signs a more specialized business—"worms" or "homemade dolls" or "original Adirondack art." This art turns out to be wooden animal cut-outs, cartoon figures at best.

There are more Shinks than any other name. In one yard, two wooden squirrels hold up a sign that says "Hazel Shink" in quotation marks, and then there's a sign painted on the side of a metal building, "Wendell Shink, welding," and then "Armand Shink" spelled out in pebbles glued to a large rock in front of a rusted blue mobile home where the lawn hasn't been mowed this year and a tree grows out of a topless car. My handyman is one of the Shinks who live in South Kilns, with no sign marking the property except "H. Shink" on a board nailed crookedly to a utility pole. His place is different from the others, completely hidden from the road behind thick pine trees. I don't know whether he lives in a cabin or a trailer, or a tent. Millie says it's an awful mess, whatever it is. She went up there last year when he was sick.

The Eagles Nest Hotel fits in with the general tone of things in South Kilns. Its blinking, sputtering neon sign juts out from a strange collision of parts: a fake pinkish stone two-story mansard box, with one tarpaper appendage on the right, a cedar shake closed-in front porch, and an old green mobile home on the left, connected to the main building by way of an open breezeway in which two old refrigerators are parked side by side, plugged in, sweating and throbbing out of sync.

Harold's pick-up isn't out front, so it's back on the bike through South Kilns, where I see Armand Shink emerge from the rusted blue trailer, an emaciated old man in a cowboy hat who waves at me, though I don't know him. I wave—then I hear a car horn, and there's Harold across the street backing the green pickup down his driveway, his head sticking out the window like a bulbous growth.

He shouts to me, "Put that bike in the rear of the truck and get the *hell* in. I'm in one hell of a hurry."

I load the bike, then open the door on the passenger side and hesitate.

"Whoops," he says, and swings the green toolbox behind the seat. "Won't be needing this baby today," he says with a wink. "So, you on your way home right now, Mr. Carpenter? Kind of pooped out? Been over to the Eagles Nest, looks like."

"I wanted you to take a look at a repair job over at my place."

"Rush order? Something about to collapse?" He rolls his arms like a paddle-wheel, somehow steering the truck with his knees.

"No. Not really."

"That's good," he says, because I gotta tell you what I got in mind for the rest of your morning, see?" This is the most he has ever said to me on any single occasion during our five-year acquaintance. And there's more: "So here you are up in the mountains and it rained for three days straight, kind of spoiled your weekend," he says cheerfully.

"Other than the puddle on the back porch, no big problem. I had things to do inside."

"More than three inches total they said on the radio. Even more rain north of here."

"Which is enough to make quite a puddle," I say, determined not to drop the subject. Harold doesn't respond.

We pass Millie's, Harold toots the horn, and we drive right by, tires screeching.

"We both know how hard it rained," he says. "Lord, I oughta, I was out in it for a couple hours fixing the roof at Peterson's. The damn rain was making a hole on the top of my head. Ping, ping, ping—you know? I should get one of them umbrella hats they have in the Enquirer, you know what I'm talking about? One of them babies." I nod my head; he'd look good in an umbrella hat. "But listen," he says, "there's something you probably don't know, unless I got you figured wrong."

"Lots of things, I'm sure." Plumbing, electrical work, and carpentry (in spite of my name). Roof repair. The essence of this conversation is that I can think of nothing to say to Harold. But because he is who he is, I don't even worry about being polite.

We turn left on an unmarked dirt road I always assumed was private, cutting north into the wilderness above Silver Lake. Wet branches flick against the pickup cab as we plow through the forest, going thirty when we ought to be going twenty. I can smell the balsam. The road crosses various little streams that have overflowed their culverts, some backed up by beaver dams. Harold curses the beavers. He says they're worse than people.

We are in the deep wilderness, the part of the Adirondacks I have always feared even as I have defended its existence among those who doubt that the wilderness even exists; my friends in Illinois picture the state as one extended city interrupted by an occasional garbage dump.

I confess (though certainly not out loud to Harold) I prefer a walk through an art gallery displaying wilderness photos to a walk through the wilderness itself. I don't like spending the night on the ground never really falling asleep, twisting to form my body around the rocks on which I've made my bed. I can't deal with the flying insect pests. Thus I occupy my mind while I avoid talking to Harold. Harold keeps his mouth busy chewing on a twig.

Suddenly he says, "Read something about these Siamese twins that were born pregnant. You hear anything about it?"

"The ones that switched husbands?"

"Different set. Switched husbands?—Jesus, who do you take me for?"

He pauses a minute, steers to avoid a huge puddle. "No, just born pregnant it said, probably not married yet. You can't be born married, can you?"

"Not to my knowledge."

"Hope not. But did you read about them, the twins?"

"No, I'm sorry I haven't read about them." Millie won't let me. "Okay." End of conversation.

We come to a widening of the road, with room to turn around in front of a heavy chain blocking our way, flanked by two identical white signs nailed into trees: PROPERTY OF CHARLES WIEGEL. NO TRESPASSING. It's like, if you can't see out of your left eye, you have no excuse for not having read the sign out of your right eye, and vice versa.

I turn to Harold, wondering whether we should proceed any further. "Do you work for Charles Wiegel?"

He says, "Nope. Never met the man. He wouldn't have no use for me anyways. This property here's nothing but woods and swamp, with just a ruined hunting camp way up at the other end of a vly, see? They wouldn't want the damned thing fixed. Tore down maybe, but anybody could take care of that. Nature could do it. I ain't been up here in many years, since I was a little kid. But I was laying in bed last night and this idea hit me. Four inches of rain would do the trick. So let's go, I said to myself, before it's too late. Life's too short."

In spite of the gaps in the explanation, I am willing to accompany Harold into the woods, to trespass on the property of Charles Wiegel—mainly to satisfy my curiosity about what he knows and I don't. We step over the chain and follow the narrowing road, with grass now a foot high down the middle and red columbine along the side as the road curves below a rocky outcrop, cuts into the hillside, and then dips to cross a brook over an old plank bridge.

Just upstream, the brook roars over a fallen beech that has become a natural dam, clogged with forest debris.

Harold is excited like a little boy. He pokes his walking stick in and out of the brook, testing the force of the water in some primitive way. He announces, "This is Shanty Brook. But this little dam is piddling. You put in a real dam, you'd see some power. Let's go, buddy. You hang around here all day, you'll miss the big show." He claps his hands, and I hop to it.

The road turns into a footpath and follows the east bank of Shanty Brook, which widens into a stillwater and then comes funneling through a narrow ravine, the sound of its passage throbbing through the woods like enthusiastic applause. While I listen for a moment, I sort the applause into individual hands clapping.

At a couple of points, we can look down over the unnamed vly, more than a mile long, the open stretches giving views of mountains I've never seen before, one of them notched at ninety degrees and shaped like a mitten.

Harold doesn't say anything as we walk along the trail. Once, he stoops down along the brook, teetering on the wet stones, and washes his face, rinses out his mouth, spits, and then takes out a ratty comb and grooms his mustache. I just stand and watch, oddly privileged.

He says, "Okey-dokey, ready to go. *You're* pretty quiet."

"I've been thinking about the pregnant Siamese twins."

Finally, he smiles. I can see it in his eyes. "You got me there, buddy," he says. "I shoulda kept my mouth shut."

I shrug my shoulders.

"Now," he says, "I can't say where I'm taking you. I want it to be a surprise, see? It won't be no surprise for me, because that happened a long time ago, but it should be a surprise for someone, or it ain't worth the trouble. Guys in the Eagles Nest oughta be ashamed of themselves, sitting there on a day like this. They may as well live in the city—to sit on their ass and watch women on TV prancing around in high-heeled shoes and hardly nothing else. So you just pay attention and watch me. And I ain't gonna *talk* much from now on because you need to listen carefully. Not a talker anyway," he trails off apologetically.

We enter a hemlock forest above the vly. As we walk quietly, I pay close attention, and hear the following: Harold's labored breathing, a seaplane cruising over Silver Lake; a bird that makes a choking noise, repeats it three times; a deer fly that I silence by twisting it in my hair.

We follow a hogback, on a dry trail cushioned in pine needles not beaten down by many boots; we are on our own here, beyond even the crudest outhouse.

Harold is pointing at his ear, smiling at me. I keep looking up at the tree tops, to see whether what I hear is the sound of the wind. But it is a windless day, and the exhaust plume fanning out in the blue sky comes from a jet plane too far away for us to hear.

We break out of the trail and turn right, through a thicket of dead trees, trampling ferns and inchling pines. It is surprising to find the forest so dead—with carcasses of beech trees strewn over the ground, and fir trees fur-less except at their very tops. It is surprising to see so many fungi. Some of the great beech trees still standing are laced by shelf fungi, white on the bottom and brownish-red on the top, some more than a foot in diameter. And on the ground, Indian pipes grow in strange profusion, white tongues of a forgotten race, dead and buried in shallow graves under the pine needles.

We could more easily go uphill, but we're cutting a traverse of the hill, digging in with the edge of our boots and weaving around endless blowdowns. Sometimes a rock formation catches my eye, and I think, what a great place that would be for my fantasy retreat (find this Charles Wiegel and ask whether he will sell me a couple of acres!); but a shaft of sunlight reveals the density of the deer fly population, and I change my mind.

The rock formations become a continuous wall, then a broken, turreted rampart in which small trees have found an opportunity, their exposed roots reaching down the rock face and grasping at the smallest pocket of soil. The wall grows to forty feet high and then curves to form an irregular ledge—over which the water I have been hearing pours in a wide cascade, a dozen separate falls. Corresponding to the size of each falls, I can hear at least a dozen separate musical notes.

Harold clears his throat. "Well, we got here in time for the big show. I gotta say it's just the same," he says, probably smiling behind the mustache.

Same as what? I merely think this question, but he answers it:

"It's the same as the day it musta been thirty years ago when I brought Margaret up here, see? You'd think some of the rock would of wore away." He goes over and touches rock.

"Great place," I say. Who is Margaret?

"But Margaret and me, we were looking for something else—supposed to be a treasure left up here by an old hermit, what Millie Hartmann told me about at school, though I knew the treasure wasn't nothing but a fairy tale. Millie used to make up stories for Margaret like that, stop her from yelling all the time. Then they decided she couldn't be in school no more, and she's been asking to go back ever since."

He stops talking and twists his mustache.

"Margaret heard the falls before I did, couldn't say what she wanted to say, just waved her arms and pulled at me, like she meant, 'Come on, Harold, let's go over there and see what it is.'" Harold pulls on my shirt, as if I were reenacting his part in that long-ago scene. Margaret is his sister; I remember Millie mentioned her. Harold lets go of my shirt and says, "Now that I think of it, I'm sure it was the happiest day of her life. You ever met Margaret?" I shake my head no. "Well that's possible. She don't get out that much, see, because she can't do many things for herself. I'd of taken her on this hike if I thought she could do it, but she can't breathe right. Once a year or so I take her out to buy clothes. Nothing real fancy, but nice enough. You should take a look at her, she dresses herself real nice. Pop, he don't get out at all."

In bits and pieces the family history comes out. He doesn't tell it as a tale of lost opportunities and deprivation, but I understand it that way. I wonder what goes through his mind as he takes care of the fancy places on the Gold Coast of Silver Lake—with their libraries and music rooms and hot tubs and heaters going all winter just in case someone wants to drop in. Even my humble cabin has to be a quantum leap over where he lives.

He hands me a picture from his wallet, dated 1957—of Harold and Margaret sitting back to back in a child's wagon. Margaret is about ten, normal looking; Harold a little younger—and, just as Millie depicted him, a beautiful, blond angel; a less trusting sort would accuse Harold of having stolen this photograph from another family. Someone has made the children smile for the picture. In the background is a long dark wooden building with a sign over the porch: WOODHULL LODGE.

"Nice picture, Harold."

"We used to live there all the time. We had our own rooms. Mom and Pop ran that place 'til it burnt down. Pop fell off the roof trying to fight the fire. I could show you the old foundation sometime if you like." Another hike; maybe.

I'm sitting on a rock shaped like a couch, in which there is space for another person. Harold is clearing away the natural debris at the base of the falls.

He shouts, "So how do you like Margaret Falls?"

"It's great." I really mean it.

He laughs as if to mock my enthusiasm. "You come back in a week and there won't be a trickle even. Well, maybe a trickle, if you come up and squeeze the moss on this rock." He's showing me how. "That's what I found out when I was a kid. We came back the next week and it was pretty near all gone. I didn't know it depended so much on the rain. I'd come up anyway by myself sometimes when I knew there wouldn't be much. Just that year, you know; never after that. I'd squeeze the moss and drink up what was left." He twists his mustache as if it were moss. "I guess I didn't want nobody else to have any . . ."

"But does anyone else even know . . . ."

"Hell no." He turns toward me as if to lecture. "They don't have Margaret Falls on any map, see? They don't put things on maps that only last a day or two a year, if they last that long." He pauses, then adds in a broken voice, "Some years been so dry, you know the falls ain't running, the moss ain't even damp, there ain't even a damn *deer fly* buzzing around waiting to see if he can get a drink. That's how bad it is sometimes."

I might have felt pity, but I think this shiver comes more from the chill of recognition—of a kindred spirit trying to make its accom-

modation with mutability, always hoping for exact re-creations of
the best moments of his childhood. I'm no different, though I come
up every year to my camp on Silver Lake to re-create an idyllic past
that never was.

But already I think I hear the musical tones shifting as the volume
of water decreases. One cascade, rope-thick, begins to whip inter-
mittently as I watch, its tone interrupted for a split second, then
resumed on a higher pitch. A ghost waterfall.

I can feel the invitation coming, but no thanks, I don't want to go
back and visit at Harold's place, where I imagine his father, a
toothless broken man confined to a living room chair, and the age-
less Margaret roaming about waving her arms at the blank walls.
Leave that part of the adventure to my imagination. I expect I'll
pick up a wilderness magazine at the store and spend the rest of the
day reading and rereading it on the porch, dodging the raindrops,
thinking, "Come fix it whenever you can, Harold."

I'm so relaxed that I drift off to sleep. I wake up. Harold is over
behind a balsam taking a pee; I can hear that extra note. One strand
of Margaret Falls has gone out of business while I wasn't looking.
And the others are pulling back. The musical chord grows
impatient, dissonant in a westerly breeze punctuated by the attack-
whine of a deer fly.

THE SKILL OF SILENCE

1986 The wall between our rooms is thin masonite, and under the cabin's gable ceiling the top is open, allowing light and sound and cigarette smoke to drift freely from my brother's room to mine. After midnight when he puts out the light and his last cigarette, only the sounds disturb my sleep—the dog's chain jingling as he changes positions, and Steven knocking his fisted hand against the wall while he dreams, the way he did when we were young and our bedrooms had a common wall. I used to think he was sending me a signal, but he never was.

When he knocks, the dog barks twice, the second bark almost apologetic, as if to say he realizes he has mistaken this knocking for an intruder. Steven pats the dog's head and says, "Good boy, go back to sleep."

The dog looks very much like the one we shared thirty years ago—black Lab, graying on the edge of the muzzle, nose up in the air when he's outside patrolling the lakeshore. My brother has even given him the same name—Bear. The difference is that it's *his* dog, not ours, and when Bear swims with us in the lake, he goes to Steven exclusively for reassurance and instructions on retrieving sticks.

"Go to Jonathan. Go to Jonathan." Bear doesn't know me, and will not go to me. He won't obey when I tell him to back off from his confrontations with "Wolf," the Chandlers' German shepherd from just up the lake. This Bear is not as amiable as the Bear from our childhood; this one tries to snap off my finger when I toss him a cold hot dog. Steven laughs when he scolds him.

All night, Steven and his dog snored in their room. I tried to separate the two levels of snoring, tenor from overlapping bass.

They went out at six this morning for a swim.

When they exploded back into the cabin, I couldn't tell at first whether it was Bear or Steven who made the choking sounds, the deep coughing, the retching sounds.

"Go outside, Bear. Do it outside," he says. Sure, Steven: blame it on the dog. The screen door flaps loudly and the dog gallops into the woods, his neck chain jingling. But the coughing and choking continue inside the cabin, toilet flushing, more coughing, then cigarette smoke as things calm down and the heavy breathing slows.

"Jonathan," Steven says. "I know you're awake. I'm going to build a fire in the Franklin Stove."

"What's the matter. Water too cold for swimming?"

"Oh no, water's perfect. But your cabin's a freaking ice-box. Aren't you going for a swim?" He clears his throat and spits in the toilet.

"It rained all night and my only bathing suit is out hanging on the line."

"You want me to get it?"

"No," I say. "That's the reason I'm not taking my dip this morning. I don't want to put on the cold bathing suit."

"You never did." My brother, one year older, has kept track of the many challenges I never took up. There's more coughing and spitting before he talks again.

"Jonathan, how much did you say you were paying for a month in this cabin?"

"Not very much really. Don't worry about it," I say in a whisper.

"Speak up! Everybody's awake."

"A thousand," I yell.

He flushes the toilet. "You make more than that in a week, anyway, don't you?"

"No. What do you want for breakfast? I'll get up in a minute."

"So you've got money left over. Have you thought of buying a nice boat?" he asks. "You could afford a very nice boat with a motor. Saw one yesterday I thought you'd like over at North Bay." All I have at the dock is a restored guideboat, which Steven calls "the antique." He can't use my guideboat because of "an old shoulder injury from football." Steven played football; I didn't.

He flushes the toilet again and the pump starts up. I think he flushes the toilet seventy-five times a day because he likes the noise of the pump, which I hate.

"I've got oatmeal and fruit salad," I say. "I'll get it ready."

"Suit yourself," he says. "I'm walking to the store."

"Pick up a half gallon of two percent milk," I say just as the screen door slams.

"C'mon, Bear," I hear him yell outside, clapping his hands. "Let's go for a walk, buddy. C'mon. Go for walk?" The dog barks wildly. God, I hope Jack and Mary Chandler aren't trying to sleep. It's only seven-thirty.

I lie in bed, pinned down by ugly speculations. The most immediate is that Steven will put another pack of cigarettes on my store account, more likely two or three. I nearly flipped when I saw the word "cigarettes" at the top of the current page of my bill. And he'll forget to pick up the milk, or he'll substitute whole milk or heavy cream.

I wonder whether that would be the right thing—to tell Millie it's *my* bill and that *I* control what will go on it. Make her establish a new store policy and pretend that it applies to all her customers: you can't charge cigarettes, beer, heavy cream, chocolate chip cookies, whatever is bad for your heart.

She probably thinks Steven and I share this account, but Steven and I made no such arrangement. I came up here two weeks ago, before he did, just to get settled down. Steven and his dog are my guests at Silver Lake. I am paying the bill. I don't mind if he charges the milk and other groceries to my bill, but if he wants his cigarettes, he'll have to plunder his own pocket.

To explain how this got started, Steven's visit at Silver Lake: we hadn't talked in two years, and then he wrote in April, saying how he knew I would be renting at the lake again this summer, and he wanted to see me before he went into the hospital. Not serious, he said. Just something that needs to be taken care of—the old football injury. *Can I bring my dog?*

Just you and the dog? What about . . .

Sarah's going to summer school

The kids . . .

The kids are traveling with friends.

So I told him to bring the dog. We'd catch up on everything that had happened in our separate lives. I assumed he was curious about what I was doing, but here at Silver Lake all he wants to talk about is the news, what we read in the four different papers he brings back from the store every morning. The cabin's a mess from the week's worth of papers he won't let me throw away.

I'm on the dock when he returns from the store.

"Jonathan, can you come up here a minute?"

"Sure. What is it?"

"Want you to watch something important." He's standing on the porch holding a bag of dog food, a cigarette dangling from his mouth. Bear is pacing back and forth growling like an attack dog.

"Stay. Bear—stay!" The dog stops growling and sits like a statue, his head moving only when the bag of dog food moves.

"All right, Jonathan, the first thing I do when preparing Bear's breakfast is pour two cups of dry Purina into his dish."

"I see." He's using a glass measuring cup. The ash tip from his cigarette drops into the dog dish as he bends over, but he doesn't notice, or this is part of the recipe.

"And I'm just wetting the mixture enough so that it releases the flavor for him. That's all the dog needs. He's on a diet, so you don't add gravy drippings. This stuff is healthy for him." Steven pours Perrier water into the dish. I guess I don't mind; I don't want Bear to get sick from lake water and vomit all over the cabin, though I've seen him drinking from the shore every day. Steven goes on: "Now, we've got to do his routine the same way every time, Jonathan. Dogs are very conservative animals. They hate change, it makes them nervous, and they won't eat right when they're nervous. I know we always teased the dog when we were kids, but we won't do it any more, will we, Bear?" The dog cocks his head.

"He thinks you're scolding him," I say.

"No he doesn't. He always knows exactly what I mean. Here Jonathan, take the dish. You know how to finish the routine. The five skills."

"Lie down. Roll over. Lemme see your teeth. Beg. Speak." The routine works the same as it did with the Bear from our childhood, though I'm sure this one speaks louder; and he's fatter and more awkward in the roll-over and begging skills. Like Steven, Bear has put on weight. As the dog plunges his snout into breakfast, Steven smiles at me, as if *I* have just performed a stupid pet trick—as if to say, "Good for you, Jonathan!" Or Steven wishes to imply that he has rendered a great service by keeping our childhood alive in the form of the dog: "Hey Jonathan, let's be happy, we've got Bear, we're still little boys!" But when I look at Steven, I realize how far we've come—even *fallen*—from our golden childhood. At forty-five, he's bald, but uses a "comb-over"—parting his hair far enough to the side so he can slick up the side hair to cover his baldness. And Steven must wear a corset when he's fully clothed because I don't see the stomach in all its grandeur until he strips to go swimming. Without his corset, he unleashes a forty-two inch beer belly, and try as he will, he can't suck it back in. He wears his bikini bathing suit too low, under the main bulge, so he probably thinks he's only a 36 or a 38.

I'm not being critical; I just understand what this fall from childhood entails, because I've gone through most of it myself. I'm losing my hair. My gums are receding. I gained weight a few years ago, then came down with dysentery while I was working in South America, lost sixty pounds, realized I was at my ideal weight, and never gained it back. I stopped drinking beer and eating ice cream.

"Beer!" That's what it sounds like when Steven calls his dog. Comes from living near Philadelphia all your life. My speech has flattened out, I think, or at least my concept of a normal accent— and Steven's accent does not strike me as normal. Whenever he says something about America, it sounds like "Amurrica," the same way Ed McMahon says it. Did I ever talk that way? Steven has always stayed close to home, close to Mom and Dad as long as they were alive—only two miles up Susquehanna Road, always dropping by, he tells me, to mow the lawn or change a burnt-out fuse. Right out of high school, he married Sarah (about whom he offers no information), had kids—they're both grown up, out of the house. Suddenly, he's not tied down the way he likes it. Maybe that's why he makes such a big deal about the dog. It's his only commitment.

He looks at me from the couch and starts to talk about AIDS. "This AIDS business, Jonathan. It must affect the way you live." Finally, the news gets personal.

"I don't have AIDS," I say calmly. He thinks I belong to a high-risk group.

"How do you *know* that?"

"I've never exposed myself to risk," I say, looking directly at him. "Not during the past ten years anyway."

"Do you think I could get AIDS?" He's picked up the Utica paper at the store, and there's an AIDS headline, a story about doctors refusing to treat AIDS patients.

"Up here in the woods? I think you're safe. All we've got is acid rain."

He coughs in a rage. "I'm going into the hospital, goddammit! I'm talking about in a month, not getting it right now in the woods. The hospital will give me a dose of that polluted blood and then I'll get AIDS. And everyone will think I'm a freaking homo." He looks at me for a reaction.

"I think the risk of that is very small. You're not gonna get AIDS and no one will ever think you're a homo."

"You think so? What the hell, I don't even give a damn. I'll get the disease and as soon as I know I've got it, I'll kill myself and save everybody a lot of money. And they can say whatever they want after I die."

I just look at him—at this weeping, middle-aged man. I don't know what to think, except something like, "If you're going to die, please spare me the death throes"—but I'd never say that. I don't want to kid my brother when he's feeling sorry for himself.

Steven throws down his newspaper and says, "You have every reason to smile. You work for the government, and you're taken care of. But me, I haven't had health coverage for a year. If I find out it's gonna cost a fortune, I swear I'll kill myself."

Do suicides go to heaven? How about people who abuse their bodies by smoking three packs a day? Does it matter? According to "Awake," the Jehovah's Witness magazine that has been lying around the Lost River laundromat all summer, nothing really matters, since only a few thousand people will be saved in the last days of Armageddon. That's an ultimate consolation for people like Steven.

I picked up the magazine when I noticed "Can our forests be saved?" on the cover. I'm interested in that question; I'd like to think they *can* be saved, and I expected to learn how. But the article asked me to take comfort in the fact that the salvation of our forests does not matter; that the trees are dying is presented as a sure sign that "Jesus will come."

He coughs all night. The dog coughs with him. The cigarette

smoke drifts over the partition wall. The light goes on, he shakes the newspaper every minute or so, turning to the next page of bad news.

"Jonathan, I know you're awake," he says faintly from his room—at five, maybe later. My solar-powered watch has stopped. Artificial light does not recharge the watch for more than an hour at a time. But the sun is coming up through the trees behind the cabin, more natural light than such mature trees should have let through, and the loons have already flown across Silver Lake (it has no fish for them) on their way to Whitman Pond, which is spring-fed and not dying as fast.

"What is it? You okay?"

"What do you think?" Why does he speak so softly?

I don't answer. At this time of day, I feel I have an excuse not to keep up my end of the conversation. Just like a dog, I'm conservative. My brother has screwed up my sleeping schedule, and now I have every right to be nervous and irritable.

He asks, "Do I sound as bad as I feel?" I could say he sounds like his wife (ex-wife?), because when the bottom drops out of his voice, that's what he sounds like. I try to think of another answer.

I look at the early morning haze inside the cabin, and give an answer to a question he did not ask: "Steven—you smoke too much."

He clears his throat and pauses before saying, "You know, I've gone on and off three different diets so far this year. Fit for Life, Pritikin, Richard Simmons. Nothing worked. Then I try to eat what you're feeding me, and I get this heartburn. Something is tearing up my guts night and day, like I swallowed a monster. I don't mean to deprecate your hospitality. You've been nice enough." After another minute, there's a crashing thud, as if he's fallen out of bed, and the cabin shakes as he runs to the bathroom. The dog gets up, shakes his chain, and whimpers. Then I'm treated to the sound of coughing, choking, and vomiting, in random order. When will it end?

The toilet flushes. The pump goes on. Steven collapses in his bed. I manage to sleep in spite of the chainsaw-saw style snoring that sounds as if it's cutting though the wall next to my left ear. I let the chainsaw cut through to the past, to the buzz of motorboats on an Adirondack lake. When Steven and I were young, we tent camped with our parents—here in the Adirondacks mostly, places like Golden Beach, Lewey Lake, Moffitt's Beach. The first dog named

Bear always came along. Mom and Dad made Bear sleep outside, but Steven would sneak out at midnight and untie him from the tree and bring him in. We'd put him between our sleeping bags. I'd tell Steven, "He'll shake his collar and they'll wake up," and Steven would remove the dog's collar, and then I'd say, "He'll run out of the tent to chase a chipmunk and never come back and nobody will know who he is when they find him without any collar." Then Steven would grab the dog and hug him all night, let him out at the crack of dawn. Bear wouldn't run off as I'd feared, but he'd sniff around the trenches of the tent to find his way back in, and Dad would wake up and think a real bear was on the loose, and he'd say, "Lorraine, where'd we put the food? Did we lock it up in the car? I think there's a bear rambling around outside the tent." By then, I remember both Steven and I would be giggling, but one of us would eventually serve time for letting the dog run loose. One punishment was this promise: "When we get home, the dog goes to the shelter. If there's one more incident like this, I swear I'll get rid of it."

Or when Bear started howling, tied to the tree at our campsite, when we left him alone so we could walk the entire perimeter road—"Why can't we bring him along," one of us boys would ask, and Dad would answer, "If he gets in a dog fight, it's all over. We pack up and go home. Does that clear up the situation?" So we'd hear him howling as we left. He could start up that way just from hearing the twelve o'clock whistle at the firehouse—places like Moffitt's Beach or Golden Beach, where the firehouse was only a couple miles away. We'd hear him making that sound halfway around the campsite.

1987

A branch knocks against the back wall of my cabin at Silver Lake, startling me out of an ugly speculation—that Steven knows my Mastercharge number and has been ordering various items over the phone. He's not here this summer, though his dog is. I'll get to that in a minute.

The dog barks twice for no discernible reason. The branch knocks again and the dog barks twice. I nod my head.

I've found out there's a special device to stop dogs from barking and howling; I saw the ad in a *Sports Afield* from the laundromat. The ad shows an electronic box attached to a dog collar, under the headline, "Too Much Barking?" It goes on to suggest that a man can teach his dog "the skill of silence." Sounds like the most severe form of behavior modification; if the dog barks, he gets an electric shock from the device on his throat. Two hundred dollars plus postage.

The dog barks to go out, and I respond perfectly.

Bear's response to *my* commands is mixed at best. I'm just beginning to learn how to get him to come and to stay—those two skills. But I can't make him shut up. He's out there on my dock half the day, baying like a wolf as if Steven had died and deprived Bear of his only link to nature. But as far as I know, my brother is still alive, no worse than last summer, though dog-less now in his new apartment. "Go to Jonathan." If Steven *were* to die, I guess Millie would clip a message to my account book, and I'd find out while I was paying for my paper and loaf of bread.

I pull out the desk drawer to go through last year's carbon copies (she always tears them out of the book and staples them to the tally, to show she's honest). Did I remember right? Did Steven really charge cigarettes to my account? Not that drawer. The one below, but the drawer sticks in the humidity, then comes flying out to bang the wall. The dog gallops up from the lake to bark at me ferociously. Who *am* I anyway? In Bear's view, I am an intruder, or I am nothing at all.

ANCIENT HISTORY

*D*avid

This happened a long time ago at Raquette Lake, camping in a tent. Before we grew up and made a lot of money.

Angie

We're not at all like the Harringtons.

We eat when we're hungry. We go to bed when we're tired. We get up when we can't stand the smell of the tent canvas any longer—you know, when it gets really hot and you think the tent might melt and cave in and smother you. When Pa wants to take down the tent at the end of the week, I stay inside until the last minute, so I know what it's like to have a tent start to cave in on you.

Some days, when it rains—but not too hard, because if it's really hard, then the trenches fill up and we've got a miniature Death Brook flowing inside the tent—some days we never get up. Pa goes fishing on those days. You see him outside under the tarp by the picnic table trying to twist into his poncho. Pa's really fat and I watch him for a long time, and he doesn't know it. A lot of people that I watch don't know I'm watching them. Pa leaves for fishing long before we get up even on a bright sunny day. Ma's giving him breakfast—I mean, a *real* breakfast, bacon and eggs, pancakes, oatmeal. When she finally thinks of us, maybe around nine o'clock, she says, Well kids, are you gonna get out of those damned sleeping bags today or not? If not, are you planning to die of starvation? The hell with you.

Ma's a Baptist, I think, and I know Pa's a Catholic. We never go to church.

David Harrington told me he was a Methodist. Maybe that explains everything—Methodist, methodical, everything at the same time every day. If I really needed to know what time it was, I could

walk by their campsite and see what they were doing. Bridge with
the Connovers starts at 2 p.m., exactly. But the time should be unim-
portant when you're camping.

If Ted and Billy and I actually crawl out of our bags and make it as
far as the picnic table, then we have a terrific choice of cold cereals
lined up on the oilcloth. I always end up with Special K after Ted and
Billy grab the Sugar Smacks and the Sugar Pops. They don't even
bother to pour the milk into the box, they just open the box and pour
it into their mouths and wash it down with Tang, and then they run
off somewhere like wild animals. That's not the way to do it, I tell
them. If you're not going to eat your cereal right, then you should let
me have them. You guys could eat sawdust for breakfast.

So then, after breakfast, I guess we've gotten up to the point where
the sleeping bag has cooled off and it's too clammy to get back in. I
take a walk.

David

At about that point in time, the grocery truck comes through
Golden Beach Campsite. It's the one from the Raquette Lake Supply
Company, and it's really a bus that has LONG LAKE SCHOOLS
still painted on one side.

Sugar daddies are ten cents. Sugar babies are ten cents. I try to
have money left over from my allowance.

Sometimes Angie and Ted and Billy are there at the same stop.
Angie buys a Baby Ruth. Ted and Billy get candy cigarettes, with the
name brands slightly misspelled—like SALAM and MARBORO.
The Dinadios have their tent at Number 202. They sawed the branches off a large tree right in front so they could nail up a stack of
paper plates. One paper plate has their last name, one has their town
("East Glenwood"), one has the names of the parents—Betty and
Gene—and each kid has a separate paper plate. Angie drew a chipmunk on hers because she believes they're almost human. "They
have souls and if I ever hear you killed one, I'll kill you," she told me.
The Dinadios made Chinese lanterns out of their old Dairylea milk
cartons, by splitting them partway down the seams, and they string
them along the tarp line—shows how long they've been here by the
number they have strung up. They're proud of it; they've been here a
week longer than we have. At night they have their kerosene
lanterns on until midnight. Angie says it's to scare away the bears.

Their campsite is down by Death Brook, the stream that flows in from the Bear Dump. We call it that because that's where the bears come to feed, and once I got to feel a bear cub's heartbeat, because it had been shot with some kind of drug and was tame. The ranger was tagging the cub, and he said, "Let's hope the mother isn't anywhere nearby. We'd have to kill her." Half of me wanted that mother bear to show up.

The latrine is midway between our camp and their camp, and there are ten camps in between, all numbered, all even numbers. It wouldn't be that much fun if we were right next to each other the way we are back home on Orchard Park Drive. We'd have to hear Mr. Dinadio farting all the time. We can't hear it at home, because he does it indoors.

I know we'd hear more than we wanted. There was a loud family next to us—they just packed up and went home. The kid my age wouldn't stop playing in the car, honking the horn, slamming the doors. We all laughed when we heard the father say, "Anthony! How many times I tell you? Huh? How many times? No desserta for a weeka!" My mother got mad at me though when she heard me say out loud to my sister, "No desserta for a weeka!" The people hadn't left yet. They were still loading their car.

Sometimes I say dirty words like "fart." It's worse to say the word than to do one, so I make sure my mother isn't around when I say it. My mother's never heard a loud fart in her life, and she doesn't want to; even a little one sets her on edge. All right, David, she always says, do you have to go to the bathroom? It's not a bathroom! You can't take a *bath* there. The correct name is LATRINE.

Our latrine is on a little hill, I guess so the water won't flow right through it and down into the stream and eventually into Raquette Lake where we swim. On the side of the men's latrine is a crooked pipe shaped like a crank—bent twice at right angles. It kind of hangs there loose; I bumped into it at night once and I could tell it was real loose and I heard a splashing noise inside the latrine. Wow! I told Ted and Billy about it and they wanted to see how it worked the next day. So Billy grabbed hold of that pipe and started swinging it back and forth, and you could really hear the water and crap in the tank under the latrine splashing around. You could also hear men yelling from inside the latrine. The men weren't down in the tank, but this was one of those old latrines where everybody sat above a common tank, and when one guy's crap hit the water, everybody else could hear it; and I suppose, if you wanted to hold a flashlight and look down you could see other people's crap hitting the water. I did that once, out of curiosity, and all I could see was the waves circling out when they splashed.

But all these guys were yelling, "Hey! Who's doing that!" And we could hear the stall doors slamming, so the three of us ran into the woods. Nobody ever caught us, but I worried for a long time about going to reform school.

It was much more scary, though, when I met a bear on the path to the latrine. That was four years ago, and my father still talks about how I looked as white as a sheet, and how they had to "pry" the information out of me—one word at a time, I suppose. Because of that bear, my little sister Janice has to have my mother take her to the latrine every time, and she's nine! She's small for her age, so it's not too embarrassing.

My other sister Christine is only three and she wasn't born yet when I saw that bear.

Angie

Mr. Harrington is also my social studies teacher. Eighth grade history. In addition to being my neighbor across the street and our almost-next-door neighbor when we go camping. For some reason they never take the campsite right next to ours.

Mrs. Harrington teaches home economics in high school, so I haven't had her yet, maybe I won't. I'd rather take shop. I can't do that, but I think they let you take typing instead, if you don't want home ec. I want to be a writer when I grow up.

Or an artist. Maybe I can take art next year. I have filled two Grumbacher sketch books this summer. All the pictures look the same, because I keep drawing the same mountain—the one on the other side of the lake. I'm trying to get it right. West Mountain has two ridges in front of it, and when I look at it with binoculars, I can see the fire tower. Mr. Harrington and David and Ted and I went by canoe to the foot of that mountain. We hid the canoe in the woods and then climbed to the top. The ranger and I had a big fight over the name of a mountain we could see from the top. He was showing us what was on the map and how we could look along the metal pointer and see the individual mountains exactly where the map said they

would be. We were doing fine until he said, Now look at that mountain right in front of us—that's Nigger Head.

I said, It can't be!

He said, It's been Nigger Head for as long as I can remember, and
I've been working this tower for thirty years, and my pop before me.
How long have you been up here watching that mountain?

Only a minute, but. . .

So you're the expert. . .

The map says *Negro Mountain*.

Oh yeah, he said, Well, that's wrong. I'll write to them and have
them change it.

You're a bigot, I said.

What's that mean?

I don't know.

Then when we were going down through the trap door to get out
of the observation cabin, the guy dropped the door on my big toe. I
was ready to kick him. Then I took some pictures on the way down
the tower. They always turn out awful. We could see Blue Mountain twenty miles away, and I thought it looked like a shrine to a
god. That could be the reason it came out fuzzy in the picture. The
gods forbid that we take a picture and they interfere with the light
in some way.

We came to a ledge, an overlook. I yelled my name across the
lake: MARIA ANGELINA FRANCESCA DINADIO. We always do
that. The Harringtons don't, but Ted and I always do.

David

Sometimes I hear her name echoing over the lake—MARIA
ANGELINA FRANCESCA DINADIO—when I'm walking by the
shore early in the morning before the motorboats start up. It isn't so
precise that I would know her exact name from hearing the echo, but
I know it's Angie letting the whole world know who she is. No one
else would do something like that. She goes on shouting her name for
an hour, it seems, while I try to zero in on her. Once I found her in a
tree. She had nailed steps into the trunk on the side away from the
road. She's thirteen now. I'm eleven, but I'm small for my age; I'll be
twelve at the end of the summer. She looks like she could be my
mother, because she's tall and has breasts.

She has her own science class during the summer while we're up at

Golden Beach. It takes place at the end of a path that goes up towards the bear dump. She's the teacher, and the students are Ted, Billy, Janice, and me. One lesson is plants (Ted got poison ivy). Another is animals (her pet chipmunk bit me). The third is human beings, and she once almost stripped naked for it, but she got scared when I asked if the ranger often came up that way. This is very valuable information, she keeps telling us, and I wonder where she got it. I think she made it all up.

She already told us this impossible story about a castle on one of the islands.

Angie

Don't scream. Pa doesn't like to be waked up once he's gone to bed. Chrissie, eat that marshmallow. I bet it's cold by now.

A lifeguard told me this story. Not Don, my boyfriend, but the college boy who was here last year. Brandon.

There are several islands near Raquette Lake Village. The big island has always been wild, no permanent human settlements anyone knows about. The people that have camps on the island now are actually robots, if you want to know the truth. But that's another story. The big island has many forms of wildlife, some species that developed independently because they were on an island. There are foxes with pouches like kangaroos, striped bears, loons with fur, and others. Some of these are extinct, and all that remains are skeletons. Brandon and I went exploring when he wasn't on duty. I wanted to take some of the skeletons but Brandon said it would be illegal. Anyway, Big Island is not populated by human beings as we know them.

The island with the church on it used to have a castle, during pre-Christian times. The church was built using the castle foundation and some of the ruins. This was over a hundred years ago, when Christians first arrived at Raquette Lake.

They built the church on the castle foundation. I already said that.

Back when it was a castle, the pagan people were fighting a war for control of the lake. It was a fierce battle, and in the end the people who lived at Golden Beach lost, and they were taken prisoner on the little island. A slave ship took them across the lake to their prison.

Among the prisoners were a family who had pitched their camp very close to where we are sitting right now. They had gone down to the beach for a swim. Actually, they had no idea a war was on, and there was no sign on the beach warning them about it. They were just on vacation, the same as us. The children knew they weren't supposed to swim outside the white buoys, but they were naughty. The parents weren't looking. I guess they fell asleep on the beach. When they woke up, they looked for their children. But the children had disappeared.

You see, what happened was the kids were just learning how to swim underwater, trying it out. They could go under for a few seconds, maybe three seconds, before they would get scared and come to the surface. Three children, all very young. And they did a very bad thing, a very unlucky thing. It is unlucky for three children in the same family to be underwater at the same time. Remember that rule the next time you go to the beach. Anyway, the enemy came and pulled all the children into submarines at the same time while the children were underwater. Then the parents ran out into the swimming area, because they saw a lot of bubbles where their children were supposed to be. And they got pulled onto the submarines, too.

Don't ask. I'll tell you. There aren't any more submarines on the lake. The State won't allow them. Other lakes have them, though, so you have to be careful.

Anyway, the family was put in prison under the castle, where they were kept as slaves for almost a hundred years. When the church was built, the builders checked the foundation and there were skeletons of some prisoners, of course. What they had never expected was to find two very ancient people still alive. A man and a woman—still in their bathing suits from when they were children.

David

So Chrissie wouldn't go swimming for the rest of the week and my mother had to give her sponge baths in the tent.

And Janice told Dad the story of the castle. I wouldn't tell; I never tell on Angie.

Dad said he wasn't surprised. Angie got very excited in class when Dad covered ancient history. She was particularly interested in pagan people, the fall of the Roman Empire, the Vandals sweeping across Europe. She even did a special report on it.

Mom and Dad play bridge all day with their friends, the Connovers. The Connovers come from Syracuse, and we know them
only from camping at Raquette Lake. They're older than Mom and
Dad, but not as old as Grandma and Grandpa, sort of in between.
For as long as I can remember, they've arranged it so they have the
campsite across the road, the first two weeks of July. I go over there
and watch them play, and eat their bridge mix. It's the only time I
can see my parents acting different, like happy. And they're not so
strict, making us ask permission to breathe, it seems.

"Mom, I'm going out in the canoe with Ted."

"Oh, that's good," she says. "I'll bid a no trump."

"When's supper?"

"The usual." My father hums gleefully. Mrs. Connover cackles
like a witch.

"Can I eat with Ted and Billy?"

She snaps out of her bridge trance and looks at me. "I don't think
so. Isn't it always hot dogs over there?"

"Not all the time." I know I'm not going far in the canoe if I have
to be back for a five o'clock supper. That's in an hour.

We get out in Death Brook, where it makes a small bay into the
lake. You have to drag the Dinadio's canoe to that point. The
wind's really coming in strong, so we have to fight the waves to get
out into the lake. I see Angie sitting on her rock, not calling or
anything, just staring out towards the big island, I guess. She
doesn't move at all, hoping to be captured.

Angie

When they pack to leave, I'll be up here looking at West
Mountain.

FEEDING ON WORDS

Randy was in his pickup making another run to the Silver Lake town dump for his mother. This stuff was so bad it had survived eight garage sales, so she'd given up on it. He tossed a vacuum cleaner, a dead lamp, a rickety chair, a soiled mattress, and then he thought he saw a familiar object in a mound of discarded appliances —an old Kelvinator refrigerator. It might have been the same one.

He remembered the first day at Pinehaven camp, when his sister opened the door to the refrigerator and screamed.

He came running in from the yard, saw the rotting venison, and said, "Figures."

"What?"

"Kevin Shink lived here all winter, then his Dad kicked him out. Looks like he forgot something." Johnny Shink had owned the cabin until March, when Kurt and Jill, who lived in the city, bought it for a weekend retreat. The younger Shink still lived in an outrageous trailer a half mile down the road—with rusted cars, Christmas decorations, three-legged dogs.

"What are you going to do?" she asked. "Where's Kurt?"

"God, I don't know," Randy said. "Do you want to keep this refrigerator or what?"

"Oh, I don't know," she said. "Kurt and I are on a zero budget."

"Then keep it."

"If that's what you want . . ."

"As if I *owned* this place . . ."

"You're always welcome to visit . . ."

"Thanks." Randy winked at his sister just as she turned to run out of the kitchen pinching her nose with her fingers.

So they kept the refrigerator and Randy removed the venison, lifting it out with a shovel and balancing it on the blade as he sidled out the door. He flung it into a grassy area between the camp and the garage and then dug a hole and buried the mess.

It had been funny back then—with elaborate burial rites as soon as Kurt returned, and a cleansing ceremony within the cabin, accompanied by incantations and a generous spraying of Lysol, the sort of details with which Kurt and Jill had always colored their lives, and of which they had begun to run dry less than five years into their marriage. Later that week after they had returned to the city, Randy had gone back in, hooked up the water, and thoroughly washed out the refrigerator. Eventually, they put a six-pack where the venison had been, and stocked the shelves with good things, and invited friends to demolition parties and plastering parties.

Now, five years later, the place belonged to other people, and Kurt and Jill were no longer together; and it seemed that only Randy had remained the same, with the same house and same job teaching sixth grade at Silver Lake Union School. The same bachelor status. Jill was out in California, in law school. Kurt had finally dropped out of grad school and was working at some shady job—phone solicitations, or driving-school instructor.

The camp had finally been sold after a year on the market, during which time Randy painted the exterior, mowed the lawn, cleaned the Franklin Stove; and as much as he felt he had earned a share in the proceeds, he kept quiet. Perhaps the money had gone to cover the high cost of the divorce—if so, it was money well spent. He had not talked to Jill about the whole affair; and their mother, who lived close by in a nice home on the south shore, would not tell him what she knew, which reduced his thoughts to speculation and memories.

The new owners sent Randy a note asking whether he could check the utilities before they moved in. It seems Jill had told them to consult her brother on all such matters, as if he had retained responsibility for this camp by living only four miles away. The camp would remain his in a sense that could never be turned to a profit. That would mean, in the long run, nothing but trouble and bitterness. Looking after other people's camps had started out as a hobby, a favor, but was now turning out to be a headache—the sort of job Harold Shink usually did, but they didn't want to pay anybody.

So on the way back from his dump run, he stopped in at

Pinehaven to check things out.

The camp was set back above a vast front yard, not really on the lake, since the property was cut in two by the Shore Road; and on the other side of the road, the land wasn't completely theirs (the new owners') but had to be shared with three other property owners whose camps were hidden back in the woods on a parallel road. These people had "beach rights" here and sometimes spent the day on the dock, noisily asserting those rights.

"Pinehaven" was spelled out in white birch twigs glued to a brown board nailed to the trunk of a maple tree. There were no pine trees in the yard, so this must have been a very old name, or wishful thinking, like many other things connected with the camp.

The building stood one-and-a-half stories, with dormers on the upper level, bringing sunlight to rooms that Kurt and Jill had never quite gotten around to fixing up, and where, finally, Randy went in and put up dry wall, at least to give a sense of finish when they listed the place with a realtor. On the lower level Jill had added a few nice touches—painted the wainscoting, installed stained glass in the window between the kitchen and dining room, and created bookshelves under the stairs.

As Randy got out of his truck, he saw the welcoming front door—the pine-cone and acorn wreath that Jill fastened to it the first summer they stayed at Pinehaven. "At least, we'll have pine cones on the door!" she had remarked. The pine cones had come from Randy's front yard over in North Bay.

He bent over and picked up price tags from the yard sale his mother had conducted on the Pinehaven grounds earlier in the summer. Randy had driven by and glanced over, and his mother waved to him from a rocking chair she had already taken for herself. He would not stop, because he still resented Kurt and Jill's throw-away attitude towards the past they had shared with him. And didn't he, in a sense, own the large dresser he could see out of the corner of his eye—the one he had worked so hard to restore five years ago, stripping the heavy yellow paint and cartoon decals, sanding, buffing, and rubbing with linseed oil? He would have no part in these proceedings. When his mother had asked for his help, he had given her the names of a couple of local high school boys who could lift heavy objects and who needed the work.

An expert at cutting the prices at just the right time, his mother had sold everything in the yard. As Randy opened the front door at Pinehaven, he realized the camp would be empty, with nothing sealed away like the surprise venison.

First thing, the water pump needed priming. He found a plastic bucket on the side porch and filled it at the stream where Kurt and Jill had built a stone dam to form a small bathing pool. (Kurt and Jill never swam down by the waterfront, because of the murky water through which they said their arms and legs looked green.) Randy took note of the small beech tree that had fallen into the pool. This was something for the new owners to take care of, requiring none of Randy's mechanical skill, and perhaps offering an opportunity for cooperative labor.

After giving the pump a workout, he heard barking, and chased a three-legged dog out of the side yard. "Go on, get out of here. Nothing here for you to eat." Trotting neatly down Shore Road, headed toward Kevin Shink's trailer, the dog looked back and barked twice every few seconds, as if disputing Randy's claim.

When he put away a rake in the back shed, he found a good broom that he took inside and pushed around the first floor of the camp, sweeping up mouse droppings. The place needed a cat.

He wondered what the mice were feeding on—insulation? old newspapers? They couldn't live on either for very long, and he expected his tour of the camp eventually to yield mouse skeletons picked clean by maggots.

A trail of thin spiraled paper scraps directed him, instead, to a niche in the interior living room wall, where Webster's Unabridged Dictionary, five inches thick, now contained a system of small tunnels partially filled with mouse excrement. When he picked up the dictionary, intending to throw it into a Glad Bag with the rest of the debris, several folded sheets of notebook paper fell out. Some were blank; several had been torn into fourths, and at the top of each of these smaller sheets was printed a single word.

Five had played the dictionary game—Randy, Kurt, Jill, and two others who had almost completely escaped from his memory: Kurt's sister Erika, and her friend Robyn (?), an aspiring actress from New York City who was involved in the avant-garde musical events that Kurt and Erika put on.

The way they played that game, each player took a turn at the dictionary, looking up a word that none of the players could have known, and then writing down its true definition—to be read aloud along with the fictitious definitions submitted by the other players. It was a game they could have played anywhere; if you were coming up to Silver Lake for the weekend, why not enjoy the outdoors? These people had been oblivious to the charms of the wilderness, the hikes Randy wanted to take them on. Often he hiked alone while they slept in.

He looked at the word at the top of one of the sheets, and smiled as he remembered the day they played that game.

Robyn stopped by Randy's place on the way back from the North Bay Store where she had bought the Sunday Times and a breakfast pastry—a pineapple danish. They had driven back to Pinehaven through heavy rain. Robyn had said, "I have a cure for this weather. All you've got to do is get a terrific indoor game started and the weather will clear up automatically. Does it every time."

"What did you have in mind?" Randy asked hopefully just as she parked the car beside the camp. She reached into the back seat and produced the heavy dictionary. "You'll see."

"MUSTH."

Robyn wrote the word at the top of five slips of paper. After taking a bite of pastry, she said, "Hmmm, I think I've used this one before. I hope not, but if I have, Erika, you must immediately disqualify yourself—because there's no way anyone could accidentally stumble across the meaning of this word."

Erika stared at the slip, then pushed up the blue-rimmed glasses that had slid down her tiny sunburned nose. "Never heard of it. Looks like a misprint."

Kurt giggled as he wrote his answer. "You'll love this one," he said to nobody in particular.

Randy worked at inventing and then polishing a definition that would sound right, that would have the self-assured rhythm of dictionary definitions. He was keen on playing the game well, as if by doing so he could make a permanent gain—more wit, more social grace, a lasting friend, at least someone to write to from his isolation in the north woods.

Around lunchtime, they had finished eating the breakfast pastry, and Jill was picking at the leftover crumbs.

Jill looked very unhappy. She scribbled a couple of words and got up and went to the refrigerator. "I'm hungry, you guys, and everything in here is very boring. I'd like to know who ate all the decent food I brought and replaced it with things I would never buy."

No one answered her question. Randy thought, I could go out in the yard and dig up the venison—maybe that would appeal to her. Kurt finally said, "Hey, bring in some Fritos and Cokes and stuff. That's all we need right now."

Robyn said, "Fresh fruit if you have any."

Randy turned to look at Robyn, staring at her lips and thinking of fresh fruit. They didn't have any fresh fruit.

Kurt said to Jill, "Hey girl, it's two o'clock in the afternoon. Why are you so hungry now? You could always eat your words, your definitions. Would that make you happy?"

"No, because I'm not very good at this game," she said. "No one ever votes for the ones I write."

"But we couldn't very well do that on purpose," Kurt said ironically.

"That's not the point," she said. "I mean, I don't need to be *humored* that way. There are other ways of humoring me." She went on until her words became simple background noise.

"All right," Robyn said as she collected all the definitions for "musth," shuffled them quickly, and then read all five aloud in a schoolteacher voice:

"Number one. 'A freshwater crustacean, related to crawfish, principally found in the warmer waters of Eastern Europe.' Don't vote yet. I saw somebody voting. I'll read them all, then you can vote.

"Number two. 'A state or condition of violent, destructive frenzy occurring somewhat periodically in male elephants.' "

Everyone except Robyn burst out laughing and turned to look at Kurt, who shrugged his shoulders, then pounded his chest and yodeled.

"Please," Robyn said, "you can't use body language like that. If you do it again, I'll deduct points. Number three. 'The presence of parasitic fungi in or on any part of the body.' " Kurt inspected his underarms. Erika held her nose.

"Number four. 'A colorless liquid emitted by Cecopria moths when they hit a fast-moving automobile windshield.'

"And number five. 'A Burmese fishing vessel.' "

Kurt immediately said, "God, Jill, haven't you used your fishing vessel a dozen times before? C'mon, play the game."

"Hey, that's not fair. I'm doing the best I can. If you say anything more, I quit."

"Don't quit," Robyn said to her. "We really need you. And *you,*" she said, squeezing Kurt's arm, "I'll deduct points for that kind of thing, too." Robyn was wearing a long blue terry robe, and her black hair was absolutely straight, parted in the middle, and precisely chopped off at the shoulders.

She read all the answers again—and everyone voted, receiving one point for guessing correctly and one point for each vote cast for his or her fictitious definition. Number three won ("parasitic fungi"), and Randy got three points—two for the players he had convinced of the plausibility of his definition (Erika and Jill) and one point also for having voted for the actual definition that Robyn had copied out of the dictionary (number two). Kurt had voted for the Burmeses fishing vessel, to keep Jill in the game, and she suspected as much and was no happier than she would have been had she received no votes.

Three years later, Randy remembered other fictions they had composed on that perfect summer afternoon, when they sat indoors under artificial light, enchanted by word magic. (As Robyn had predicted, the game brought out the sun.) Even Jill, who at one point disappeared for five minutes to put on her bathing suit, never left the camp, perhaps out of a conviction that the others would continue to play without her, devising ways to mock her in their definitions; but, in fact, the game could not be played very well with fewer than five people, and the only thing that would happen if she walked out was that the others would blame her for spoiling their fun.

Randy looked at his sister Jill in her bathing suit and thought, "Uh-oh, she's getting fat."

The game went on. He couldn't remember whether they had stopped for supper. Since only a few slips of paper now remained from that day, defining "musth" and two other bizarre words, what Randy mostly remembered was the peculiar definition, not the word that it purported to define. "Peanut-butter headdress" was a favorite, something Robyn had come up with in mad desperation;

and all of Jill's variants on Burmese fishing vessels (some of which turned out to be correct definitions!); and Kurt's improperly worded fictions, like "what we do when we sit down to the table and are unable, even by great force, to pull our chairs any closer"; and Randy's own favorite invention, during a later, bawdy phase of the game—"the state or condition of being turned on by the friend of a relative." This definition had been misread at first and thought to have incestuous connotations, and then properly understood (by Robyn, who smiled slightly), and strangely misunderstood (by Erika, who stared at her brother in disbelief). But finally, everything was worked out—well, almost everything—when the author of the definition revealed his identity.

"Hey, it was me, and I didn't *mean* anything by it," Randy said, throwing up his arms.

The definition had received no votes. It achieved nothing. Randy spent his winters even more isolated than before. He wasn't any different from the dozen or so young guys who hung out at the Lost River Inn nursing a beer.

Robyn had finally said, "If he said he didn't mean anything by it, then he didn't mean anything." What would it have taken to get through to her?

He now looked at one of the other words left over from that afternoon, and wondered why nothing more had happened—what other parts were left over and exactly where.

"SALEP."

In Kurt's boxy childish script:

"A state or condition where facial hair grows inward." Randy realized that Kurt had never played this game to amass points, but to impress somebody, and Randy doubted that it had been Jill.

Erika (?): "A small Egyptian dog, now extinct." One vote.

Jill: "A starchy drug or foodstuff consisting of the dried tubers of certain orchids" (her turn at the dictionary, obviously).

Randy, himself: "A small African hut in which puberty and other secret rites are performed." There was something slightly wrong with his wording. Maybe he had been drinking heavily at that point.

Robyn (?): "A Middle Eastern dish, very hot and spicy." Next to this one, three crude pencil strokes marked it as the winner—the author had to have been either Robyn or Erika, each woman a stranger to him, except on that warm afternoon when Pinehaven had promised to be a real haven, and perhaps more than a haven, an opening to a different kind of life, as any room full of out-of-town people could be.

But something had happened the next day. They could not live on words alone, and a lengthy argument had ensued over the question of how they were going to eat, followed by the very sudden departure of Robyn and Erika in Erika's old Datsun. Followed by a long period of silence, and then some terrible food at a bar in Silver Lake.

Randy was now left to fill in the blanks and come up with his own fictions for all four names, on the order of—

1. A person who can be seen talking in the background in a commercial which is set in a restaurant or a supermarket in suburban New Jersey.
2. A wanderer, particularly in summer resort regions.
3. An overweight person who disparages junk food.

The fourth? He laughed, thinking of Kurt, and how much he had once enjoyed his company—and wrote out the definitions on a blank sheet, folded it, and was about to stick the paper in the niche. Let the new owners puzzle it out, he told himself. Why not leave scraps of notes everywhere, definitions for words and people that might otherwise have no connection to the present world? "Present world," he thought, and went to the window to see what was barking.

Then he unfolded the paper and wrote the fourth definition: Three-legged dog in search of buried treasure.

27594

THE BLUE TRAIL

Late September: the man and woman tried to sleep under a small plastic tarp, but the rough hand of the wind jerked it back and forth like a kite. At times they were covered by nothing, and they took a direct hit from the rain.

Rick looked up at the sky. The tarp was like a drifting eyelid that wouldn't blink the right way when he saw a raindrop growing from a branch, or when he thought about the power of NoName mountain looming over the Blue Trail.

Their clothes were fifteen feet away, woven with low balsam trees as if they had flown in the storm that night from the tarp line. He wished the clothes would trap the coydogs he could hear coming louder and louder, or muffle the sound of the widow-maker, the sound of two dry branches scraping together to make a howling on a distant cliff.

All night Rick smelled the plastic groundcloth, orange peels, sweaty socks, and fly dope. He was glad he didn't sleep because he'd have bad dreams.

At five in the morning, a tree branch snapped and he thought a whiff of dog breath crossed the dead coals of the evening fire. A six-inch flame for a moment.

He looked up from his soaked bedding. The sky had turned a shade just lighter than the rippled black tarp. And he could see an outline, the shadow of a huge gaunt man, or a tree with two crooked branches and what looked like a dragon head. This man-shape seemed to control the string on the kite which this tarp had become.

"Let go, man! Let go. Just let go," he yelled.

Flashlight. Transformed out of what seemed like a dislocated bone in his back. He flicked on the light and pointed the faint beam towards the crooked shape—which was nothing more than he expected, an odd-shaped tree with a huge nest halfway up. He could see their clothes still on the line, hanging limp now, soaked and heavy. He said, "Shit." Then, "Sorry." She said nothing.

He got up on his knees and hit his head on the feminine bulge of the rain-filled tarp, spilling water over the edge and onto the ground cloth..

"Sorry Kristen. Or is it Kirsten?"

She said nothing. He spotlighted her sleeping bag with the flashlight—and saw the bag was empty. Did I sleep? I *must* have slept. That was one hell of a bad dream.

Here are the important facts, Rick told himself. The flashlight battery is almost dead. The rain has stopped, but secondary rainfall from the trees is soaking my only dry clothes. The coals from the campfire might be good for another half hour of dull glow—not heat—at the most. All possible firewood is wet.

She must have gotten up a while back, she had to go in the woods. Women go more often than men. They can't hold it as well. The rain makes you go. The cold weather. One hell of a bad dream. Just a dream.

Rick called her name, alternating the two pronunciations, and the echo came back at a pitch higher than he would have liked, the cry of a loon. He thought he had frightened her, so he stopped calling. He had never wanted to frighten her, but he'd done it anyway. Or she had been driven away by one of those coydogs. In her rush of adrenalin, she had climbed a tree. He looked up, where the trees faded into a smoky blackness.

"C'mon, man, you're not making any sense!"

The Blue Trail angled up the shoulder of NoName Mountain.

Late September and cold as November. This is the version running through his mind: They had planned to stop at the lean-to by Shanty Brook, but the shelter was full, so they climbed another mile and found a level cleared space in the underbrush, a tent site others had laid out before, with a crude ring-fireplace in the middle, trenches outlining the shape of a tent, and a length of old rope strung between trees, a clothesline or a place to drape the tarp. They built a camp-fire. She brought the wood and he broke it and threw it on. It was a good fire.

And here is the story she'd told him by the campfire:

Yes, that's right. I recognized one of them back there. I guess it could be a coincidence, and the light wasn't very good. It was the outfit, the green plaid shirt with the orange down vest.

And the guy in the vest returned my look. His head turned ninety degrees, until we were out of view. God, that was frightening, but I didn't want to act as though anything was wrong at that point.

If he was who I thought he was, he still might not recognize me. He's never seen me dressed up for a hike. Dressed down. He only knows me in a dress and high heels, my hair up. I mean he's only seen me clearly in a courtroom. And he wore a suit and tie then, so it's possible I'm wrong. I'm just talking now. Don't read too much into this . . .

Pieces of my life in Colorado sometimes turn up here, not just landscapes, she said. I guess that's to be expected. After all, it's only been a year. But this would be such an amazing coincidence. Really amazing. Maybe I'm just doomed to see a face even in the most remote resemblances. God knows, I wasn't very convincing in the courtroom, and then he looked at me as if to say, "I'll be seeing you, honey." Even when I look at you, please forgive me for saying this, I have to pull back sometimes, I react physically, remembering what I had to go through back then. Forget what I just said. I'm just talking.

The last few words she slowed down, as if she didn't believe them. Rick didn't say anything. He waited for her to continue.

"Time for bed," she laughed nervously. Rick had hoped she would go along like a good sport.

Because the tarp was so small, they slept close together, but back to back, as if they needed to watch in both directions. They both fell asleep watching. He *did* sleep, and he dreamed that awful dream. The coydogs howled at night, one voice on top of the other, so that while one coydog breathed the other could keep the noise going.

Out on the Blue Trail, having failed in his search, Rick woke up lying face down in deep moss, and whatever inhabited the moss now inhabited his face. The liquid in his eyes followed the track a tear would take. His body trembled. The rain had stopped and he could see a small blue metal disk nailed into the trunk of the tree in

front of him, a marker for the trail to NoName Mountain and the
Lost River region that lay to the south. He fingered the map in his
pocket. It was wet like everything else, and he couldn't read it
anyway because the flashlight was dead. He held the dead
flashlight in his right hand, and shook it to prove how useless it
was. When he littered the woods with it, the spring and batteries
popped out like parts of a bomb. He took off his hat and squeezed
out the rainwater and rubbed the top of his head to get warm.

"Kristen! Hey, Kristen!"

Their camp was only a hundred yards down the trail, and she
wasn't there. He saw his pack still hanging like a dead man from a
tree branch, the tarp still tied up and full of water. Both sleeping
bags lay there on the ground cloth, husks of creatures that had
wriggled out in some nocturnal metamorphosis. But her pack was
gone, and so was most of the food, all the breakfasts to which one
merely added water, hot or cold.

"Someone's been here . . ."

Rick slapped his pants pockets and found his wallet but not his
keys. He shook out his sleeping bag on the ground cloth, yielding
three coins, a comb and a pair of dirty socks, still warm. He
crawled around on his hands and knees patting the ground for his
keys, but found only natural objects like pine cones and sharp
rocks. No trace of Kristen. He would have thrown something
breakable. But everything was unbreakable.

After dumping the water and untying the tarp from the trees, he
stuffed it into the top of his pack with his sleeping bag, punched it
down and tied the top flap. The ground cloth wouldn't fit, so he
bunched it up and kicked it into the woods.

"Dammit." The pack weighed a ton.

He hiked downhill toward Shanty Brook Leanto, nine o'clock in
the morning so he ate a cherry lifesaver for breakfast. Every minute
or so, he would spit out cherry juice and call out her name. And
every minute this search would get more and more ridiculous, and
other plans and options came into his mind, depending on which
version of the previous day's events he accepted.

"Kirsten? Is that who you are?"

He saw he had spit cherry juice on his right hand. It washed off
when his hand brushed a wet mountain maple.

At Shanty Brook, he found the shelter empty. He crawled to the back over the rough hemlock boughs, hoping to find something artificial. An earring would be enough. His search yielded nothing but old graffiti dating back to the 1960's, including a peace symbol carved into the wood a quarter inch deep. He ran his finger through the groove wondering what it meant; and in each pair of carved initials he tried to decide who was the man and who was the woman; and who carved it—the man or the woman. He touched "K.L." and picked at the wood on the upper half of the K until it became an R. "Serves you right," he told the initials.

Around back of the shelter, he found a pile of rusted cans somebody should have buried or removed and new cans out front in the fireplace—baked beans, peaches, evaporated milk—tossed where the next hiker would find them, crush them, and then pack them out. That was the way people did things when they played by the rules. ("I didn't carry her in.") Rick stepped on a can to see whether he could feel it through his boot. It only felt good, and he left it there for the next hiker.

He sat down on the front bench of the lean-to and changed his socks, putting the dirty pair in an old soup can. Same smell as the soup, he thought.

The consequences of her death—he reviewed them quickly.

Somebody would have to hire a new waitress.

Somebody would have to console her family.

The father of her daughter would obtain sole custody.

And Rick would have to find another set of keys. That was a definite consequence. He felt in his pocket where he kept loose change, and squeezed the coins as if he could form them into the keys he needed. Somebody had tossed Kristen in a bog, the keys were lost in the bog with her, and he would have to get a new pair. That fact made his face hot.

He would beg a ride out from the trailhead, then get a ride back with the new set of keys. He thought he had an extra set in a drawer somewhere back in Albany.

He was up and hiking again, calling her name dutifully.

"You lose a little girl?" a man asked him, the first he had met that morning. The man wore a poncho although the rain had stopped. His glasses were dotted with small raindrops.

"No," Rick said. "Is there a little girl wandering around?"

"Not that we've heard about," the man said. He didn't look very strong, the type you could get ahead of quickly. A woman in an orange vest caught up. She had long black hair and a wide beaded headband.

"Hi," she said in a calm tone. "We heard you calling. Were you calling somebody?"

"I'm just looking for a woman," Rick said. "Long blond hair, maybe in a pony tail. She was wearing jeans and a ski sweater and she had a brown pack. She has glasses but she wasn't wearing them . . ."

"Your *hand* is bleeding," the woman said and turned away to look into the woods. She didn't turn back.

"Sorry, fella, I can't help you," the man said. "We just came in this morning at Third Lake, and we haven't seen anybody on the trail. Just a group of people pulling out in a van when we were parking."

Rick stopped to think. "Did you see other cars there in the lot?"

"A couple," the man said.

"How about a white VW Rabbit?"

They both shook their heads, and the woman said, "We really don't remember. There could have been a *Rolls Royce* but the sun was just coming up." Then they moved quickly away.

Where the next stream crossed the trail, Rick looked up towards a mountain, saw a waterfall about two feet high. The water made him happy. He took a drink and rinsed his mouth. He decided he would sit on a rock in a sunny area by the falls and wait for people to come by.

He waited several hours on that rock, and almost lost track of life itself, as the sun broke through the trees and warmed him as if he were lying on a summer beach. He wondered whether a tan would make a difference. If he pulled out all his hair or combed it differently. In his mind, he figured out what he would tell people when and if they came by.

Around two o'clock, a man wearing a Smokey-the-Bear hat kicked a rock in the stream. The man looked to be unarmed. His badge said, "Henderson."

"You been down by Lost River?" Henderson said.

"Nope," Rick said.

"Elk Mountain?"

"No mountains today," Rick said cheerfully. "Change of plans. Lazy, I guess."

"Hiking out soon?"

"In a bit," Rick said, looking at his watch and noticing it had stopped at 2 a.m.

"Well then, have a good one, and sign out at the trail register." Henderson left slowly, poking a stick in the leaves as if he were cleaning a city park.

Rick remembered skiing on this part of the Blue Trail a few years back. It had been early April on an eighty-degree day, steam rising out of the hard-to-believe snow. You'd go for a while, and the snow would be great, and then you'd run into footprints and then a washout where you'd have to take off your skis or ruin them on the rocks.

Back then he had a different set of friends, people who pushed him to get outdoors and enjoy himself. One of them even tried to get him to marry her, although he had not realized it at the time. They were sitting down to lunch and she said, "I still want you." He had changed the subject, because the word "still" made no sense, and he didn't care if it ever made any sense. He often pictured her saying those four simple words, and the "still" never made sense, although he finally came to realize he had no memory for feelings, other people's feelings—so maybe something had happened that he had missed or forgotten. This was a useful realization only insofar as it explained certain words that other people spoke; it did not change the way he felt about himself.

The night had been cold, but now the temperature was in the high sixties. Rick thought it strange that on a nice day like this, he had met nobody coming up the Blue Trail. Conditions were perfect—foliage at its peak. He almost expected to see his old set of friends coming along to fetch him back to the life he had once lived. This was the sort of day when his friends went out and took a perfect hike. Afterwards, they could pack him out to civilization like a crushed tin can:

> IF YOU CARRY IT IN . . ..
> Enjoy the woods and your goodies. . .
> Leave your woods as they should be—CLEAN.
> Your empties, cartons & papers are light in weight.

Be good—Be strong—Considerate and Proud—
PLEASE CARRY IT OUT.

He moved down the trail as if he were skiing, carefully shifting his
weight from one foot to the other. The dead leaves were like snow.

He tried to remember what he had done with his knife. He hadn't
carved his name anywhere. If she had taken it from him, then why
hadn't she stabbed him first?

If it was still in her pack, would it complete the puzzle? Or was it
in *his* pack? If it was he'd have to get rid of the pack. The pack was
too heavy anyway, an encumbrance if he had to outrun somebody.
Henderson had looked lean and mean. Rick wished he could toss
the pack into the woods. But he'd be running toward Lost River,
wouldn't he?—and he'd need the food he still had, cookies, cheese,
candy bars.

By the time he had worked out answers to these questions he was
too close to the trailhead to turn around and run.

At the trailhead, the rangers waited for him with the handcuffs.
And when Rick held out his hands, he saw the toothmark on his
right thumb.

DELIVERING BREAD

I. *Summer 1981: The Thunderstorm*

It was Glenn Stanger's first summer driving a truck for Klingman's bakery. Kenny Holtzman, the previous driver, now his manager, had warned him, "Some of those women will drive you crazy."

Glenn's route took him up to the big stores in Williston and Tannersburgh first before he hit the Adirondacks—where things would get weird. By the time he reached the mountains, he was usually out of everything except white bread, so he always caught hell from the women who ran the stores up there. He couldn't believe the promises they made in exchange for more doughnuts, danish, pies, and cookies.

"Come upstairs. We'll toast some of your Cracked Wheat and put something on it . . . ."

Or, "I have this cabin. No one's rented it this week . . . ."

He was a lonely man, but he said no.

If it had been possible, Glenn would have set up a bakery in the back of the truck. But he had to settle for what Kenny gave him. And the ladies in the mountains would just have to talk their customers into buying those long loaves of squeezably soft Sunbeam bread. "Hey, you could tell everybody to put butter and sugar on it. Jelly. You'll sell more jelly."

"We don't sell jelly," Marilyn would answer.

Marilyn Shink loomed at the end of the route, and got last pick. She was the biggest complainer, one from whom any promises would be the least tempting. She knew it and she never made any, but she let him know how she felt about the situation.

Her store was part of a private campsite at Partman Lake—milk, bread, ice. The basics. A few other items—whatever you could stuff into a ten by ten shack, like souvenir plaques and obscene bumper stickers and an occasional ugly craft item on consignment. Marilyn was a big woman, but her husband was practically a dwarf, which allowed a little more room for junk in the store. Carl was the guy's name. Carl was useless, as far as Glenn was concerned. He had no discernable purpose except to come in and sneeze on Glenn when he was trying to load the bread rack.

A young, very blond girl, a lifeguard about fifteen years old, lounged on the porch as Glenn took in the Shinks' two dozen white loaves and random doughnuts and cookies. He'd see her there as he backed out and turned around (a process that took several minutes in that tight space). She would already have a big glazed doughnut in her mouth.

"My mom paid for it," she'd say.

He put two and two together and realized her mom was Diana Watkins, who frequently climbed into the back of the truck to help herself. Not to steal, but to get first pick.

Diana Watkins came over from the North Shore of Partman Lake, where the family had a lodge and a fleet of six boats, according to Marilyn. They were an old leather family from down in Tannersburgh. "None of them's done a lick of work in the last fifty years," Marilyn was happy to say.

The lifeguard daughter was the exception. He learned her name—Amber. Seemed like a good name for a cat.

Glenn was twenty-eight and divorced.

And he wasn't in the least interested in Debby Shink—twenty-five or so, unmarried, and wall-eyed. They dressed her in men's shirts and overalls and let her do latrine duty on the campsite grounds; he'd seen her coming out of a latrine with mop and pail. Then they tried to doll her up in a long dress for a party. Gave her a permanent that made her look like a grizzly bear. What a joke! He'd seen her that way one Friday afternoon on the porch, then wandering down a pathway when he'd gone over to use the campsite latrine. As a token of his pity he once left a babka cake just for her, and they'd made too much of it. Practically sent in an engagement announcement to the Williston Journal. The year-round folks up in the mountains—they were desperate to get husbands for their homely daughters.

He laughed every time he drove out through the campsite gate, the stupid sign on the arch: Y'ALL COME BACK NOW, Y'EAH. He tried to pronounce the last word the way they'd spelled it and it didn't seem right. Did they leave out a letter, or was the apostrophe extraneous? It would be consistent with the sign in front of Marilyn's store: "T"HEE CAMPSITE STORE. Kenny always referred to it as the Teehee Store, and they'd both laugh.

Glenn was still sweating from unloading four trays of hamburger rolls for Diana Watkins' dock party. "Yeah, yeah. I'll come back," he said, "but next time, I want an invitation to that dock party."

"Hey little thing under there . . ."

"I wasn't about to go to her stupid party," Amber told the breadman after he unloaded his truck down in Utica and found her hiding behind the "dead bread."

"What's the big idea?" He tried to sound angry.

She just smiled at him.

Her mother had taught her well.

"When the hell did *you* get on?" he asked, grabbing her arm to pull her up.

"Oh, you know, Glenn, when you stopped at our place with all those hamburger rolls?"

"Uh-huh." He smiled to think she had used his first name. Just like Mama.

"I mean," she sniffed, "Where *are* we right now?"

"New York. I took you all the way to New York City."

"Come on!"

Later, Glenn learned that Diana Watkins' party had been ruined by a thunderstorm, drenching all the rolls as they sat out unprotected; while Utica, in the Mohawk Valley, remained fair and sunny. Glenn could still remember what they ate in the truck, the cinnamon rolls and sugar cookies he had taken off the shelves because they had just reached their expiration date.

II. Winter 1982: The Blizzard

His winter route extended only as far north as Stewart Lake. Partman Lake would have taken him another five miles into the mountains and deeper into the snow belt—on a road that was always the last to be plowed, never in time for his morning run. Twenty or thirty people lived in Partman Lake all winter, most in trailers, but they got their bread, cake, and cookies by coming down to the Stewart Lake store, owned by John and Judy Alton.

Often on Wednesdays and Saturdays when he came up to Stewart Lake, he would find Marilyn and Debby hanging around. Glenn could feel the tension in the air—Marilyn and Judy were still feuding with each other. He knew that during the summer Marilyn would often sneak down to Stewart Lake in a wig and sunglasses and raid Judy's bread rack while Judy wasn't looking, when one of the college kids was working the register. She'd buy twenty dollars worth of Klingman's products to re-sell at the Teehee Store. And then Judy would come out and suddenly notice she was out of doughnuts, out of variety breads, hamburger rolls, chocolate chip cookies, cleaned out of everything but those long Sunbeam loaves.

The breadman insisted he was not to blame. "After all, you sold that stuff, didn't you?"

"That's not the point, Glenn. When I'm out of bread, I may as well close the store." He smiled, as though she had complimented him in some way.

"Don't laugh," she said. "We'll get another bakery to come in."

"Sure you will," he said. "Some fancy patisserie in Paris. Baked fresh every morning."

When Marilyn came down to the Stewart Lake store in winter, she bought plain white bread. "For French Toast." As many as three loaves at once, twice a week. "Well," she said, "We have to put out crumbs for the little chippies, the snow's so deep this winter and they might starve." Judy rolled her eyes the way she always did.

"Marilyn," Glenn said, "I could give you a few old loaves. I mean, for free." He pointed to the plastic tray on the floor, which held two loaves of rye bread that had gone bad, marbled with blue mold. Debby bent over and squeezed one of the loaves.

"Just like in the past, the pick of the litter," Marilyn muttered.

"Debby, get your goddamn hands off that garbage!"

Judy said, "Teehee," then covered her mouth quickly, and Glenn coughed to avoid laughing. "How about a cup of coffee," Judy finally said. "Keep you warm for your trip down the hill."

"Sure," he said.

"It's almost ready, and I shouldn't drink all of it." They heard a plow go by.

Marilyn said, "Judy, we're going now."

Debby said, "Bye Judy. Nice to see you."

"Just a second, Marilyn," Judy said, "I've had your bill added up for a week now. What do you want me to do, add it up again next week? It's a new month, and we're trying to clear all the accounts."

"Haven't we always paid?" Marilyn said. "You've got people that never pay. Never. I know Jack LeGow. I bet that account is four years old if it's a day."

Judy didn't bother to dispute the claim. She said, "Marilyn, I even hate to mention it, but John's been bugging me."

"Don't worry about it, Judy. Carl says, why worry. You'll only die young. So don't do things you hate to do."

Judy put the Shink account book back on the shelf, letting it jut out slightly so she could pull it out again quickly. "So Marilyn, what's old Carl doing with himself these days? I haven't seen him in more than a month. John saw him the other day hunting up by Moose Lake." Nobody said anything, and Glenn stared at the wall where Judy still had Christmas cards on display. No discount on them yet. "Here, Glenn," Judy said. "Have a cup. Marilyn and Debby care for any?"

Marilyn opened the outside door and said in a zombie voice, "The next time we come down it will be with a check, Judy."

"Bye now." They finally left.

Judy laughed. "If I have to wait for a check, the next time they come down could very well be June 15th, when the campsite opens and those three start working again. And you know, it's not as though they have no income during the winter. They get welfare. It just burns me up."

"I wish I could do that," Glenn said. "I lose money all winter. I may as well go on welfare."

"You do fine in the summer, Glenn. It evens out. You wouldn't want to go on welfare. John and I had to do it ten years ago and I don't think he's ever recovered, but I always say we more than made up for it in the taxes we paid."

"Yep. I believe it," he said.

"I'm not ashamed of it."

Glenn took a long sip of coffee. Judy now had two rows of Pepperidge Farm Cookies. He was worried she'd start carrying their bread, too. He didn't want to say anything about it.

He looked at her postcards—two for twenty-five cents. If he got stranded at Stewart Lake in a blizzard, he could send a postcard to his boss. "Dear Kenny, You're right. They *are* crazy. One of them is holding me hostage up here!"

There was a postcard of the lake featuring the island and a canoe on a calm summer day. Nothing taken in winter. Most of them showed kittens playing, or a deer standing in an anonymous meadow. For each animal postcard, the caption said, "Greetings from the Adirondack Mountains," but when he turned them over, he saw they were printed in California. And then there was a postcard showing the front of the store, with the rear end of the Klingman's truck ("old-fashioned goodness, a family tradition") on the right, taken before Glenn had been the driver. A sign along the top of the porch read, "Canoes. Camps. Bait." He smiled, for some reason.

His eyes lit on various reminders of summer: fishing gear piled on a back counter, life jackets impaled on a horizontal wooden pole, the extra ice freezer (unplugged, sitting there with its lid off), a stack of dusty charcoal briquette bags. The center post served as a bulletin board, with business cards, news clippings, and photos. An old clipping said, WOMAN'S BODY FOUND ON NO-NAME MOUNTAIN. Glenn remembered the State Troopers searching the back of his truck during a massive manhunt. He stared for a long time at a large color photo—a bunch of kids doing a fancy water-skiing formation, triple decker, with the very blond Amber Watkins on top, hanging on to some guy's head with one hand and waving with the other.

"How's business, Judy."

"Oh, kinda slow. You know how it is."

"Yeah," he said. "It seems I'm taking out more old bread than putting in new. I've got a truckful out there of both. I'm even taking out the good stuff you always beg for in the summer. I've got boxes and boxes of donuts."

"You don't look like you're in a big hurry to get back to town," she said.

"Not today. Take a look outside, Judy."

The Texaco sign rattled in the wind, and snow had drifted up against the side of the blue Klingman's truck. Exhaust was coming out of the rear of an old grey Plymouth.

"Now what the *hell* are Marilyn and Debby still doing out there?" Judy rapped on the window in an absurd effort to get their attention.

"Maybe they forgot which way was north," Glenn said.

Judy flashed the Genesee beer sign on and off, and the car finally left. "Well," she said. "I guess they're all right."

"I could tell you a tale or two."

"About them?"

"About anybody up here," he said, making excuses not to leave. "There's really nothing to tell about the Shinks. Those folks are just barely making it, and they do what they have to do."

"Marilyn's so pathetic," Judy said. "They're all pathetic. I think they *live* on that bread. She isn't feeding it to the chippies the way she said."

"They eat meat?"

"Yeah, they do, but they never buy it here. Marilyn comes in and fondles a package of frozen hamburger, y'know, complains about the price and then she puts it back. It's part of our weekly routine. I tell her, 'You handle that meat another minute and it'll *thaw* on you.' Then she tells me, 'Looks kind of dark. I'm trying to get it under the light.' It's just a charade. She won't buy the meat in any color."

"Then where do they get their meat?" he asked.

"I think it's whatever Carl kills in the woods. He's a poacher, y'know. There's no particular hunting season for him. It's all year, and nothing's off limits, including dogs. That's why John won't get a dog for us, even though the kids are always begging."

"Hell, I don't believe that," Glenn said.

"Believe what?"

"That Carl's a poacher."

"I wouldn't put it past him." She poured another cup for herself and showed him the pot. He shook his head no.

"They don't look like they're starving," he said. "Debby's got a nice little tummy on her. They fattening her up for the slaughter?"

Judy laughed and then stopped suddenly. "I can't believe you said that. I mean, I just said *dogs*, and I don't know that for sure. This conversation's getting a little out of hand. God!"

Perhaps Debby was pregnant. Judy didn't want to talk about it. Why did she care?

Glenn watched her fill up the wire cigarette rack. Each column needed no more than one or two packs to top it off, but she was squeezing them in. She broke open a surplus pack of Salems and started to smoke. This was new, but Glenn held back on any reaction. Kenny had told him, "Judy's not bad, just a little paranoid. She wants to know everything that's going on, but the truth is, she's better off not knowing."

If Debby was pregnant, there weren't very many men around to step forward and claim paternity. At least a couple could be in *big* trouble if they did. Half of the men in town were Shinks, and one would hope that would eliminate them as possibilities. Who else? Jack LaGow? That pathetic drunk hadn't been seen out of his trailer in the past three years. His sons were both married now and living far away. Sam Packer? Once quite active with the ladies, but now over seventy and confined to a wheel chair. Maybe it had been the new guy with the beard who drove the truck for Star Dairy, a smile on his face all the time.

"What time is it getting to be?" Glenn asked.

"Eleven-thirty," Judy said. "And look outside. I hate to tell you, but your truck is almost buried in snow."

"Yep. Well, send John out if you see I'm not gone in five minutes."

"Bye Glenn. Bring me a cheese danish next time."

He waved at her with one hand and carried the bread tray with the other as he shuffled through the snow to his truck. He set the tray on the ground and ripped open the two moldy loaves and flung them into the woods. "Some little critter will make a meal of it," he thought. He smiled to think of Debby squeezing the loaves. Maybe she was color blind, but now he was sure she was pregnant—strange cravings for moldy bread. His ex-wife had been like that, the year she miscarried.

He didn't bother to load the empty tray into the back, just stowed it next to him on the front seat.

The driving wasn't bad in the mountains. The mountains cut off the high wind, and the visibility was okay. He followed tire tracks for a while. It was when he came down on the Mapleton plateau that the visibility dropped to zero and he pulled over.

White-out. Try to be sensible. Plenty of old bread and cakes in the back, if it takes a while to clear. Run the heater every half hour. I know what to do.

He stood up and walked through the opening to the back of the truck. There was nothing back there. All the trays were empty.

AMAZING GRACE

The Timberline was one of those Adirondack bars that stayed open all winter for the snowmobilers. And even when there was no snow, they stayed open. Someone might drop by, though the Timberline was the last bar on a road that led to an empty wilderness, so empty that the State road map used the blank space for an oil company trademark.

We drove up from the city on a three-day weekend in February. My brother, his wife, and I own a small camp we've partly winterized, a few miles south of the Timberline on the shore of Silver Lake.

We like to say that we ski cross-country, but we hardly ever do. Maybe twice a winter up at Silver Lake. The skis look serious enough, racked neatly along one wall of the back entry, with a shelf of waxes, scrapers, cork, and a butane torch, but the skiing is nothing but a concept. The snow never seems right. Sometimes it's a hard crust, sometimes it's a few inches of powder over a slush base. Even under the best snow conditions, we need to put up five or six bridges before we can use our illegal trail. Once we dragged a log bridge over from the old State snowmobile trail, which was closed because it didn't lead to any bars.

That snowless February a few years back, instead of skiing, we stayed inside to work on the camp. Jeff was making twig furniture and Janice was arranging hand-made tiles in a pattern along the front of the hearth. We were all singing. I'm the youngest member of this group, maybe the most musical, but the least skilled in arts and crafts, so I contented myself with sweeping out the cobwebs and animal droppings.

As I worked, I thought how nice it was to own a camp, as a compensation for having to live in a bad apartment all year—all the noise and bad fumes and lack of natural light. Then Janice yelled, as if she were trying to make herself heard over city noise:

"Hey guys, don't we have any food for supper?"

"Is the store open?" Jeff asked.

"Look, you guys, I don't want to thaw out frozen hamburger. That's all they ever have."

Jeff said, "We could drive up to the Timberline."

Janice said, "Are they open? I don't want to go to all that trouble just to find out they're closed or they don't have any food besides beer nuts."

It was a six-mile drive north to the Timberline, along a paved highway that had been a one-lane gravel road until 1964, when Walt Partman talked Governor Rockefeller into paving it as far up as the Timberline. Walt had owned the bar then, and had been a State Assemblyman for a couple of terms, but now, in his eighties, he was retired from public life. He still lived in a big white house set close to the highway he had paved, and he still had not taken down his Scorpion Snowmobile dealer sign, even though he'd given up that business several years ago when people stopped buying.

The Timberline came into view a couple of miles north of Walt's place, right where the power line ended. The bar was partly log-cabin, with white mortar and very dark logs, and partly green aluminum siding topped by a phony mansard roof. They still had a cut-out Santa with sleigh and reindeer out front. In back, to one side, was the blue trailer where the present owners, Sam and Charlene Packer, lived—with a dozen dogs, one would guess. A white sign out front said, "Food-Cocktails."

Sam, a bald man around sixty, was wiping glasses at the bar straight ahead. Off to the left and right were two small dining areas, each with four tables; on the right in back was an old upright piano, painted white. Sam had the radio going. It faded in and out as he pounded it with his fist.

"I don't know why I don't get better reception." He was talking to us or to himself.

"What station?" Jeff asked.

"Utica."

"Sounds like it's coming from Canada. It'll come in better after dark."

"Ice storm supposed to be on the way," Sam warned us, and

coughed up something which he put in a cocktail napkin.

"Pitcher of Genny," I said. "That okay?"

"Sure," said Jeff. Janice was over sitting at the piano, touching the keys but not playing. Charlene finally came out.

"Thought I heard people," she said. "What the hell is going on? The whole town drop dead? I haven't seen a soul to talk to all afternoon. I don't include this fella." She squeezed the back of Sam's neck. She wore a pink bathrobe, and her hair was up in a green silk scarf. "Pardon my appearance. I didn't think I'd be cooking except for Sam and the dogs."

"No menu today," Sam explained. "She has to go look in the freezer."

"Okay, kids," she called out from the back, "I have pizzas —they're all deluxe, very good, we had one last night and ate it in two minutes it was so good. And let's see, a few T-bones, they'd take a while. They're like the Rock of Gilbraltar."

"Do you have soup?" Janice asked. "I think I'm coming down with a cold."

"We have Campbell's tomato in a can."

"Okay."

Jeff said, "And we'll have the pizza. Are they large?"

Same held out his hands a foot apart. "Like so."

"Two of those."

Charlene said, "I can make you kids a lettuce salad. Or how about a chef's salad, my specialty. Chunks of ham and cheese. Won't take long."

Janice played ragtime on the piano. The radio signal was completely gone.

"Where'd you learn to do that?" Sam asked. "That's pretty good, missy. Wish I could do something musical, but a half dozen of the keys on that damned piano don't go down so good unless you hit 'em with a hammer."

"They're not part of the song," Janice said.

Looking out the window, while Janice started up on another ragtime piece, I could see Charlene tiptoeing in her slippers across old snow toward the blue trailer.

A pair of black and white dogs jumped up at her out-stretched hands, thinking she had treats for them. But she just had them up to keep her balance.

"She needs a few things from her own kitchen," Sam said, bringing the pitcher of beer to the table.

Janice played "The Easy Winners."

Jeff said to me, "I gotta talk to you about something."

"Oh yeah? Right here?"

"Can't do it right now. Maybe we can take a walk later."

"What's wrong?"

"Oh, nothing serious."

"Can we make you kids sing for your supper?" Charlene said. She set down the large Tupperware salad bowl and then brought over the soup.

We were embarrassed. I finally said, "At home, we always used to sing a blessing—'For Health and Strength.' "

"Oh, I don't want to hear that," she snorted. "I get my religion three days a week as it is. Do something like what you would do in a concert."

Janice didn't look as though she wanted to do it. She stared at me in an odd way as if I knew the answer to an important question.

I said, "We could do 'Amazing Grace.' It's the best thing we do without instruments."

"Go ahead and use the piano," Charlene said.

"I think the piano's a half-tone flat," Janice said, poking at middle C and shaking her head. "I didn't bring along my pitch pipe. All right, Mike, do you have a C?"

"Sure," I said. I can usually get it closer than a half-tone, even a quarter-tone. My highest note is an octave above middle C, which I can hit under ideal atmospheric conditions. It's like a mental barrier I can always reconstitute as the same note.

Sam brought over the pizza and sat down with Charlene at the next table. I gave Jeff his note—middle C, a "bagpipe" note where he stays for almost the whole song. He varies it with dynamics. Janice took the G, a fifth above, for the melody. Then I took the C an octave below Jeff. There was another note we couldn't include, unless Charlene, with her raspy basso-profundo voice, could somehow be trained to sing mezzo.

> *Amazing Grace, how sweet the sound*
> *That saved a wretch like me.*

> *I once was lost, but now am found,*
> *Was blind, but now I see.*

The text meant nothing to the three of us, but Charlene applauded it. She believed in faith healing, and went to a little Pentecostal chapel over in Cedar Lake where they spoke in tongues.

"I wish we could get our little church choir to sing like that," she said. "Of course, there's only one man in the choir and he's almost deaf." She turned to Sam. "You know Frank MacGregor, used to be married to Wendy? He's been coming to church service the last three months." We were already eating. Charlene kept talking, in almost a whisper, which was ridiculous since the only other creatures who might have overheard were a stuffed weasel and a stuffed martin perched above the bar. "I'm not gonna go into all the details of how he lost his hearing and such. Because I don't know everything about it. They got a place over in Lost River, five miles from here. *Had* a place. Well, Frank's still there, you see the light on at night. They both used to come up here most days and drink till closing, and they ran up quite a tab. I don't know where they got the money to pay their tab, but they paid regular. You wouldn't think they made very much selling firewood and having yard sales, would you? Or whatever it was they did to stay alive. So I don't know. But anyway, they always got stinking drunk. And she got very loud."

We were on our second pitcher. Jeff gave me a questioning look.

Charlene continued, "The both of them are in their forties. Maybe not even that old. Well, I hope not! Her mother and me were only a couple grades apart. Hazel Shink had Wendy when she was sixteen or seventeen. So we're not that old, ha! ha! I'd always say to Frank and Wendy when they got up to leave, 'Are you two gonna be all right? Do you want me or Sam to drive you home?' And they'd be all right, because, you see, they only drove ten or fifteen miles an hour and kept the car on the shoulder all the way home.

"That would have been okay, but their tail-lights went dead and they didn't do nothing about it. Couldn't come up with the money, probably. So they had their little accident. A car came up and knocked them into a tree, and both Frank and Wendy went flying into the windshield. Not through it, but they both took quite a bump on the head. And they went into the hospital down in Utica. Walt Partman drove them down, since there's no ambulance up here.

"Now I'm gonna tell you something a little strange. The bump on the head had a different effect on each one. Frank started going deaf, and he got religion, found Jesus, and joined our church. Wendy, on the other hand, she became . . . Sam, you old rat, this is *not* funny, so just wipe that smile off your face and go wash the dishes. He thinks this whole thing is funny. In my view, good and bad came out of it. And, what got me started on this? Oh, yes, well, it brought Frank to the Lord, but it brought him as a deaf man, who wanted to sing, but he couldn't."

A man came into the Timberline. We all looked up, expecting Frank. It was a young man with long blond hair and a beard.

Sam said, "Hi, Greg."

Charlene said, "You want something to eat?"

"Nope."

Charlene looked at Sam. He didn't say anything. He didn't move. The young man sat down at the bar.

Charlene got up and said, "Greg, you *know* what the sheriff told us. I don't know why you keep coming around, when you know I'm not gonna give you nothing. And Carol said you been bothering her down at the store."

"She won't even sell me a quart of milk."

"Is that it? Do you want a glass of milk?"

"No."

"Then I'm sorry, boy. I can't serve you."

The young man gave each of us a look, Janice a good hard look, and then he walked out, making a hard hammering sound with his heavy boots.

"Well, there's another case," Charlene said. "His grandfather was a forest ranger, a hero to the boys around here, if you can believe it. I don't know what's happening to the families around here . . ."

We were back on the road after scraping the ice from the car windows. I drove. Jeff sat beside me and Janice was in the back. She pulled a sleeping bag over herself and said, "I'm wiped out."

Jeff said, "I'm not."

I said, "I hope I'm not," and my brother looked at me as if to warn me again.

"Hey Michael," Janice yelled. "Aren't you going to turn on the heater?"

"It's on already."

"You're full of it. I'm freezing to death back here." And she was drunk. She started to sing. "Amazing grace . . . ."

We joined in, ". . . how sweet the sound," putting on all kinds of swooping embellishments. We sang verses we didn't even know. Secular verses, obscene verses with bad puns.

On Peck's Hill, the car started accelerating near the curve to the right that swings around Walt's place. I could see the fan of illumination, a car coming the other direction. A small particle of fear started to work within my system, and I put on the brakes, lightly. And the fear did not really increase as we went into our spin, never leaving our lane, not even brushing the horn-squealing van coming the other way.

We stopped skidding and sat in a daze. Our lights now pointed north, fixed on the south side of Walt's house. Nobody said anything. There was just this huge photograph of Nelson Rockefeller, blown up, like a billboard—that had been fastened to the side of Walt's house for as long as we could remember; and below the huge smiling photo of the late governor was a sign that read, "THANKS TO MY PAL."

HEAT AND HOT WATER

Greg's 1969 white Valiant backfired and sent up a wake of brown slush as he drove past Kenny's place, on his way home with three bags of groceries he had bought in the city. He worked for Kenny, but didn't buy his groceries from him, because he didn't want Kenny and Diane to watch him spend his paycheck. They already knew him much too well. They probably knew what he was doing right now, even what he was thinking.

The problem was his kid brother Scott lived in one of their cabins and ate meals with them. Scott was just out of high school, two years younger than Greg. Both boys worked for Kenny, who installed and serviced furnaces and plumbing systems at camps all around Moose Lake. Kenny and Diane also had a small grocery business, a motel, and several winterized cabins. When you said "Moose Lake," it was Olmstead's that you meant—the metal building with the store and the plumbing and heating business side by side, the cabins, the motel, the brick ranch house where they lived. There was nothing else for five miles either way on the main highway, except signs that told which way the highway curved and where the rocks might fall. All the camps were off the highway on private roads. Until Greg went to work for Kenny, he had never seen any of these camps, although he had lived two miles up the road from Moose Lake all his life.

In the rear-view mirror he could see Kenny in his blue ski cap carrying a box across the highway from the shop to the store. Greg thought of a sign they could put up here: You are now leaving the village of Moose Lake, population 7. You are now approaching—well, there wasn't any name for the place where Greg lived. The mailing address was Rural Route 1, South Kilns, New York, 13852; and South Kilns, a hamlet of fifty people, was more than five miles away.

No name for where he lived. For years, people had called this cluster of cabins and trailers "Robersons," which was his mother's father's name. Grandpa Roberson had been the State forest ranger for many years, a tall man with a handlebar mustache and a badge, respected by everybody. He had disappeared in the woods when Greg was in fifth grade.

There were no more Robersons, and Greg's father, Jack LeGow, had made a name for himself as a notorious drunk and all-around loser. Once a world-class speed skater, a member of the 1956 Olympic team, he was now sick and fat, and seldom seen around Moose Lake. There had been a time when Jack LeGow had been highly visible in Iroquois County, tearing apart various bars in the early morning hours, racing his car along Route 27, showing off in the motorboat he no longer owned. Nowadays, he hardly even got out of bed, and Greg had gone weeks without being aware of his father's existence. In fact, most people who had known Jack LeGow in his prime thought he was deceased.

There wasn't even a sign to mark the LeGow settlement, just three mailboxes: Jack LeGow, Greg and Linda LeGow, Helen Rogers.

"Scott," Kenny said to Greg's brother while they worked in the shop. "When you gonna get married?"

"Don't know." Not soon, he thought, not if I have anything to do with it.

"I'm not pushing you, believe me. If you were to go out and get married, I'd lose a good worker. And then I don't know what I'd do."

He thought about the implications of what Kenny had said. First, Scott would leave if he got married; that was true, since there wasn't anyone around here he was interested in marrying. All the local women seemed to be missing teeth, and they smoked too much, and they had dirty hair. Or Kenny meant that Scott wouldn't leave, but because he was married, he wouldn't be as good a worker—like Greg, whose marriage probably affected his work. He wasn't sure that was it, but Greg always seemed to have problems with his wife. He never went into any details, except to say, "Linda's having a bad week," whatever that meant. Scott felt exempt from certain generalizations that might apply to Greg, for unlike his brother, Scott had finished high school.

Kenny said, "Didn't I see Greg's car go by a while back?"

"He get his car fixed?"

"Engine still sounded bad. I did give him a couple hundred in advance pay for car repair. Just an investment in getting him to work on time. I can't have the guy thumbing rides to try to get down here in the morning. He has to be here at eight o'clock, or no job."

"Did I tell you my Dad's car is up on blocks? He hasn't been out in ages."

Kenny didn't say anything for a while. Scott figured he didn't care much for his father, but who did? Then Kenny said, "You know, there's only one car every ten or fifteen minutes on Route 235 this time of year, and not every one's gonna pick up a hitchhiker that looks like a hippie."

"He's not a hippie." There was a long pause.

"A Hell's Angel."

"No motorcycle."

Kenny didn't say anything. He blew his nose. "You saving for a car, Scotty?"

"Not for a car. Maybe college tuition?" It was like he wanted his boss to say it was okay for a guy like Scott LeGow to think about going to college.

They were taking new parts out of boxes and entering the inventory in the computer. Kenny let him work on the computer. Scott knew he wasn't as good as Kenny's older boy, Tim, who was in seventh grade and an obnoxious genius. But he was certainly better than Greg, whose fingers were blunt and uncoordinated, who could hardly dial a phone; who was okay for lifting two hundred pounds of cast iron, but not for handling wrenches and screwdrivers. Kenny had seen that right away and kept him away from anything that might break. Other things about Greg weren't so obvious. Scott wondered whether his brother could even read. That was how well he knew him.

"So that's how you're gonna leave me," Kenny said in a joking tone. "Gonna go off to college and leave me in the lurch."

He didn't answer, but he knew Kenny'd do okay without him, and he knew he couldn't work here forever, even though it was nice. The Olmstead boys were growing up. Kenny was fifty (ten years older than Diane) and eventually would turn the business over to one of the boys, or put it on the market. Either way, Scott couldn't tie his future to this business, even though it was a profitable one right now, as the people on the lake began to upgrade and winterize their camps.

Every step he took was a way of avoiding the foolish trail his brother had blazed. In school, he knew he wasn't the brightest, but he asked for extra homework and projects to improve his grade. When he graduated at Silver Lake Union School, he made the top ten percent of his class (third out of thirty-one), and he hadn't let it bother him that no one from his family watched him walk across the stage to pick up his awards. Or, later, even mentioned his graduation. That summer, Kenny had hired him and given him a place to live, plus meals, and Scott had begun to believe he wouldn't turn out exactly like his brother, as his father had predicted in one of his drunken rages. And then Kenny's business had expanded in October and he'd gone out and hired Greg, who was married and on welfare. Scott wondered how long that would last.

Linda was somewhere around. Greg could smell her cigarette smoke, and her kids weren't back from school yet. That was good. He liked them okay, but they kind of drove Linda into hysterics these days, and he always had to leave the house and walk in the woods for an hour, go cross-country skiing back on the Silver Lake trail. He didn't own a snowmobile yet.

"I'm in the bathroom," he could hear her calling.

"Okay."

He put away the groceries. Four cartons of Salems for her. Boy, they were getting expensive, but she went crazy when she didn't have at least a week's supply of cigarettes in the house. Greg didn't smoke anymore. He got enough smoke just by breathing hers second-hand. He put the cigarettes on top of the cupboards, where the ten-year-old couldn't get at them.

Five gallons of milk. You couldn't get the plastic gallons at Olmstead's store, and their half-gallons cost almost as much as a full gallon from the Price Chopper—a dollar twenty-nine. A gallon a day, every day, Greg and his family drank milk. Next door, his parents never drank milk. Closest thing was non-dairy creamer for his mother's coffee. One look at their garbage can was enough to tell you how things were going—all potato chips, cat food, and beer. Greg himself was a "non-drinking alcoholic," and went to

A.A down in Williston.

Next summer, if he was still working for Kenny, he'd probably stop in and buy milk from their store. He'd go over to the deli case and ask them to slice a pound of bologna, try their potato salad.

The damn kitchen was too small. There were toys all over the floor that he tried to kick out of the way, but he kept tripping over them, and he swore at them as though he could scare them away like animals or children.

"Who the hell are you talking to?" She was still in the bathroom.

"Nobody. Are you taking a bath or what?"

"No. How could I? When the hell are you guys gonna put in the hot water like you said you would?"

"What?"

"Hot water. We don't have any fucking hot water. Is there something wrong with your ears? Maybe if we had hot water, you'd wash out your fucking ears. Can you hear what I'm saying to you? Greg? Say something."

He didn't answer her. Let her rant and rave. It was true he had promised to look into the possibility of overhauling the bathroom, but he had been afraid to bring it up with Kenny when he'd only worked with him less than a month. Maybe in a couple of months, after he'd proved himself. In a couple of months, he'd have a real handle on this job, and he'd feel comfortable asking for Kenny's help.

He sat down at the table and pushed the dirty dishes out of the way. He didn't want to guess what she'd had for lunch. Too many dishes—most of them full of ashes. You could always heat the tap water in a pan. The electricity was still hooked up.

"Greg, I said, *hot water.*"

"Yeah, I know."

"You get the car fixed?"

"I think so."

She came out of the bathroom looking pale and shaky, trying to tie the belt of her robe without much success. Thirty years old, and sometimes she looks pretty good. Today, she looks all dried up, really old.

"Greg, you better be goddamn sure about that car. I'm driving into Utica tomorrow, and I don't need any car trouble. So, on my way, I'm going to drop you off at Kenny's place. Is that all right?"

"What are you gonna do in Utica?"

"Buy new clothes."

He laughed. She didn't need new clothes. They both knew she was lying. She never went out, except to the local bars around Moose Lake and Silver Lake, where a flannel shirt and jeans were all you needed.

She took her long hair and started brushing it, looked at the brush, frowned, then took a rubber band and pulled the hair tight into a pony tail. Her hair was flat and dirty, getting thin along the hair line—and as a result, her forehead looked enormous. Greg turned away and stared out the kitchen window. He could see Helen Rogers on the porch of her trailer, in her light blue robe, tossing scraps of bread to the birds. With her hands up in the air, her torso turning from left to right, she looking like she was dancing.

Scott stayed at the dinner table talking with Diane while Kenny moved to the living room to watch the weather on TV. Three of the boys were doing their homework, and a computer printer screeched in the background.

Scott looked at Diane's mouth when she talked. She had all her teeth, and they were all white.

"What do they have for heat out there?" she asked. Diane had never gone up to LeGow's; she didn't get along with his mother for some reason. So she asked him questions about how they lived.

"Do you mean my mom and dad? They have baseboard electric heaters in most rooms. There's practically no insulation, so those heaters are going all the time. They spend half their income on electric bills, I think." He was embarrassed to refer to their welfare money as income.

"I know what you mean. Of course, we have the best equipment since that's our business, but we're trying to heat several buildings all winter. It adds up."

Scott asked, "Should I turn down the heat in my cabin?"

"Oh, no, don't be silly. You keep it much too cold in there. When I go in to clean, I have to wear my down vest." She smiled at him. "And when I clean, I don't find much—no more than a couple of dust balls in the corner." He liked her a lot, and couldn't believe she was almost as old as his mother. Her voice was very smooth. He had never seen her lose control. For that matter, he had never seen Kenny blow up or anything, even at Greg when he most deserved it.

"Greg and Linda just started to put insulation in their cabin," he said. "They used to have electric heat, but they switched to Kerosene because Niagara Mohawk keeps sending them shut-off notices. It hasn't been shut off yet, but they're getting prepared for when it is." In a way, he wanted Diane and Kenny to know how desperate they were, though he was ashamed to talk about his family.

"Maybe they'll stop here to buy their kerosene. I don't know where else they'd buy it."

"Maybe they will." They'd better.

Kenny shouted from the living room, "Batten down the hatches. Blizzard coming."

Scott went into the living room to look at the TV weather map. There was a big white blob over the eastern part of the country.

Kenny had the two-year-old Bradley sitting on his lap feeding from a bottle. He said, "Does your brother have snow tires on that car?"

"Not that I know of. He usually puts weights in the trunk."

Kenny set the baby down and started making a phone call.

"Your brother have a different number now? Unlisted? I can't get through to him."

"Greg doesn't have a phone anymore. He told me they were going to get a short wave radio. They don't have it yet; they're saving for it."

"That's just plain stupid. What are we supposed to do? Send him messages through your parents?" It sounded as farfetched as routing messages through Russia.

"Please don't call them, Kenny. They'd just hang up on you. Why do you need to call my brother?"

"I don't want him to come to work tomorrow. I won't need him since I'm not going out on any jobs. Not in this weather. We'll stay in the shop and finish up inventory."

"He'd think he was being fired."

Greg woke up in the morning knowing he had forgotten an important item on his errands the day before. Kerosene. They were down to a couple of gallons, or maybe less. Linda didn't know about it, so she hadn't yelled. She was sitting up and smoking in bed. She could keep warm by smoking. He could hear the TV in the next room, and figured the kids had gotten up.

"Do you think you oughta smoke in bed?"

"I'll smoke whenever *and wherever* I damn please."

"You're not going to Utica today," he told her. "I won't let you. Just look out the damn window."

She didn't do as he said. She got up and went in the bathroom.

He looked out the window again. He had to keep wiping it with his hand. There was a light on in his parents' trailer, and he could see his mother's head in the kitchen window. It was moving around in an odd way. Then it left the room, dropping diagonally, and the light went out. Greg felt an overwhelming despair. He began to feel as though he would swing his arms wildly, breaking things left and right. He grabbed his right arm. What was there to break? A couple of ugly lamps; one mirror, in which he saw his cockeyed face. He sat down on the bed, still in his pajamas. Very soon, he would cut his hair, shave off his beard.

Then he heard the town snowplow go by, and his mood lifted. Got his keys and wallet from the top of the dresser. He put on three layers of clothes over his pajamas and checked the money in his wallet. The wad of bills—two hundred dollars—was still there.

When he walked out the door he didn't even turn his head to look at the children, nor did they look at him. The TV could keep them going indefinitely. His wife hadn't come out of the bathroom. That was good.

"She'll still get her welfare," he thought. "She can get a divorce and have welfare. She can have everything but the car."

He had new snow tires, the best Goodyear super radials—so he just drove out, without even shoveling. A man's voice was yelling in the trailer, but Greg didn't stop to think what it was about.

"She could make car payments if she stopped smoking."

When he drove by Kenny's place, he didn't even wave at his brother. But Scott held his hand up as he stood out in the parking lot; he looked like he was about to wave or he was trying to get Greg to stop. Doing neither, Greg made the engine roar as he left Moose Lake. He had only one thing on his mind—he was thinking about how he would look with short hair.

OLYMPIC

At night, the blue neon sign flashed "Olympic"—"Pool"—
"Coffee Shop" two seconds apart. But Paul Chester knew his way
home without the help of the neon sign. Walking to his father's
motel for his first meal of the day, Paul stepped on the coarse gray
remnants of a snowbank that had been four feet high at Christmas.
He simply followed his own deep footprints, clear down to the mud
and gravel.

Just before the big curve on Route 235, the sign for the other
motel in Lost River—the "Matterhorn"—was half burned out,
spelling the word "Matter." The Olympic's only competition was
slowly going out of business, as each letter expired. Even if the
building disappeared, Sandy and Jack Getter could leave up the
sign, because it would still apply to something.

Sandy sat in a chair and Jack lay in the bed in one of the many
unoccupied units at the Matterhorn.

"You'll come up with the answer," Jack yawned.

"The hell . . . I don't have any more ideas," she finally said.

"Dance around. Make it snow."

"Snow wouldn't solve everything."

"We could burn down the Olympic," he said.

"Sure. And then we'd be even *worse* off. We'd just be this
lonesome little motel all by itself up the road from a charred ruin of
another motel."

"Yeah, I know, I was kidding."

"Sometimes I wonder," she said. She flicked her lighter and held
it two inches from his red-bearded face. She should have set his
beard on fire, but the only thing that happened was his pupils
dilated. Then she lit her cigarette and got up and walked to the

front window. A car actually drove by, which made her laugh—
because she didn't recognize the sound of the tires.

She looked at Spruce Mountain across the way, the last patch of
reflected sunlight near the top. She could see the Edelweiss trail—
just a zigzag of snow, a bit of lightning in the sky. The mountain
seemed higher than it really was, and it made her dream and ignore
the sad reality of Lost River Ski Bowl: a six-hundred-foot drop,
seven trails (most novice and intermediate), only one with snow-
making, one double chair, one J-bar. Not what you would call a
destination resort. Hardly anyone outside the county had ever
heard of the Ski Bowl, and the Town was talking about closing it
down. Paul Chester would be out of a job.

But in the early seventies, there had been talk of a new highway,
with passing lanes on the hills, a more direct route north from the
Mohawk Valley to Lake Placid back when they had started to pro-
mote Lake Placid as a future site for the Olympics. (And now,
when the LPOOC had actually pulled off the miracle, Route 235
was full of potholes and went nowhere, and the Olympic torch
would be carried up another highway ten miles east.) Sandy and
Jack had bought the place on her small inheritance back in the good
old days, when they were just out of college and wanted to make a
life for themselves in the Adirondacks.

The white patch on the mountain went dark, and Sandy turned
away from the window.

She wasn't sure what she wanted now. It would be enough for
the moment to change the pictures on the walls, to put up scenes
more in keeping with an alpine resort. Why were there paintings of
Mexican bullfighters? Who had done that? Jack? It seems he didn't
know a thing about running a motel; his heart was never in it, and
she suspected he went around from room to room hanging bad art.

The mirror was crooked. She knew better than to look directly
into it, but caught a glimpse of the definite cowlick in her hair;
opened a dresser drawer as if she'd find a comb there. All she found
was a sheet of emergency numbers, none of them current.

Jack was practically asleep on the bed, but she couldn't figure out
why he was so tired.

"Well," she said. "I don't know what to say at this point. Because I
don't think you're serious. You keep falling asleep on me. I know this
isn't bothering you the way it is me. Go back to sleep, little baby."

"Okay, so you wanna go over to the Olympic and talk with Paul?"

"My God, you're awake!"

"Come on, let's go see Paul," he said, rolling over on his stomach and pushing himself up to a kneeling position alongside the bed. He looked like he was praying, but he wasn't, because he didn't care enough to pray.

"You don't want to talk about this anymore," she told him.

"Hey, that's not what I said."

"You want Paul to tell us what to do," she said.

"Oh, I don't know. I just wanna be with people."

"All right. I'll go with you," she said, and put out her cigarette on the dresser top.

When his glasses defrosted, Paul saw five customers sitting in the Olympic Motel Coffee Shop. He had no idea who they were—young people in cable-knit ski sweaters, Norwegian sweaters with geometric borders. Locals didn't dress that way. Couldn't afford it. You'd wear a heavy shirt or two, with a down vest to keep the chill away from your heart, and let your arms and legs freeze, more or less.

Usually all you'd see in the Coffee Shop were the locals who lived at the motel, like Minnie Rogers, eighty years old and wearing her usual black wig, who had lived above the Lost River General Store when there had still been a general store; or Kathy Shink, under-dressed in a sleeveless blouse, who was trying to keep a safe distance from her husband Kevin, a violent drunk who hunted and trapped out of season. Wendy MacGregor—the less said, the better. It was nice to see new faces, since the fifty people who lived in Lost River all year recycled too frequently and didn't get old or weird fast enough to make it interesting.

He might go over to the newcomers and tell them about the special deals at the Ski Bowl. He had discount coupons in his shirt pocket for guests staying at the motel, weekend packages, great bargains. Then he thought, why push it; if they can read, they'll know from looking at the signs on the wall—mixed in with ski posters from much more spectacular locations than Lost River. Paul stared at the real Matterhorn and daydreamed; he had never even been to Colorado.

Paul had put up a snow-conditions chart by the door—depth and snow-type. The depth said SIX INCHES (which was an exaggeration). The snow-type said GRANULAR, MACHINE-MADE. While he looked at the door, Sandy and Jack burst into the room and headed for his table. They almost made the place look crowded; Sandy was small but took up space for two or three people, always moving around.

"Okay Paul, you gonna treat us to a beer?" Sandy yelled as they sat down. Of course he would treat them; more than a year ago, they had given up the pretense of running a tab at the Olympic. Paul's father still knew what they owed him and kept the receipts in the office.

"You guys eat yet?" If not, Paul didn't mind treating them to a meal and a beer. "The chili's good. Just go over and take some out of the pot, my compliments." He thought, "Dad doesn't have to know."

"Haven't even thought of eating," she said.

"That so?"

"I mean, my stomach rumbled a while ago and I said, 'I hear you. Now shut up,' and then I put it out of my mind." She didn't get up, but Jack went over and helped himself to the chili.

"So you two are busy over there," Paul said. To be busy was honorable, even if one wasn't making a lot of money.

"Sure," she said, blowing her nose.

"No vacancies?"

"C'mon, you know! Almost *all* vacancies," she said. "I think we have one person staying with us."

"Who?" Jack said, swallowing and clearing his throat. And why? Paul thought.

Sandy looked at Jack. "Isn't there a salesman in number twelve?"

"That was last week," he said.

"I oughta send over Kathy Shink," Paul said. "I think by now, Kevin's figured out she's staying at the Olympic."

"Don't do me any favors," Sandy said.

"Or ole' Minnie. Minnie might enjoy the change . . ."

"She'd fall down and sue us."

Paul looked at Sandy and thought, "You'd better be willing to take in welfare clients if you want to stay in business." Obviously, the tourist trade would not keep the Matterhorn going. He swallowed the last drop of his beer. "So if you're not that busy, what have you been doing?"

"We've been wracking our brains, Paul." Sandy looked like the brain-wracking had messed up her hair. She used to have nice long hair ten years ago when they were in high school.

"Yeah? About what?"

"Trying to figure out what to do next. Tomorrow. Next week."

Paul wondered why Jack was silent. Depressed, maybe. What would they do when they went out of business? Not if, but when. Who could be conned into buying that pink elephant? The State would have to take it. Of all the ugly buildings along Route 235, the Matterhorn was the most tragic—sitting over there with its half-dead sign, phony chalet roof, pink stucco, plastic balconies. It wouldn't even look right in Storytown. The property itself wasn't bad, though—two hundred acres stretching back over the mountain into the wilderness, once you got past their junked pickups and snowmobiles. He'd skied it with Jack and he wished he owned the land. Some day, Paul would have to move out of the Olympic; maybe things would get so bad even his father would go out of business and Paul would end up living in a trailer. He knew he'd always have a job in Lost River, because he worked for the Town and the Town itself would never go out of business; even after all the buildings rotted away, there would always be the roads to plow and the taxes to collect. But he was afraid the Town would shut down the Ski Bowl this year and they'd put him on the road-sanding crew.

He said, looking at Jack, "Did you ever think of putting in condominiums?"

Sandy answered, "Not now. That's over. Yeah, sure, five years ago, we looked into it. We used to sit in the kitchen and make sketches of what we wanted. Until the APA said we couldn't, because our land was Resource Management and we already had the maximum of three buildings or whatever it was."

"It's more than that. And you could get a variance," Paul said.

"Dream on," she laughed. "I'm sure the APA wants Lost River to turn into a ghost town, like Powley Place, which is a little dot on the map, but nothing more than a meadow when you drive by. We'll be like Powley Place in ten years. The State will see to that." She took out a cigarette and lit up. "I'm telling you it's hopeless to try to get the land re-classified."

"Except to State Land," Paul said.

"Yeah, that's true," she said. "The State wants to put together a cross-country ski trail to tie in with the Northville-Lake Placid Trail. That would be something, wouldn't it? Maybe not. I don't know. We've already got the ski loop over by the river, but that's not enough." She coughed. "Something different anyway." She was trying to draw a map on the placemat. "Look, the highway comes within eight miles of the trail near the old Lost River School. They'd have a trailhead there. Ask Jack. Jack went to the meeting." Jack heard his name and snapped out of a daze.

"I didn't tell them," he said, "but I already got my own trail going over there. Damn, I wish it would snow so I could use it."

In August, Jack Getter had walked every day in the woods by himself—on the back property of the Matterhorn along the row of red-slashed beeches that marked the edge of State Land. Then one hot afternoon, wanting a hike with a view, he took out his ADK guidebook to check the description of an abandoned trail not far from Lost River. The guidebook had said, "The view from Hogback Fire Tower is shortened in almost all directions by mountains nearly as high as Hogback, so it is not surprising that this tower is among the many the State has closed. There is no view without the tower, so the closing is unfortunate, because there was a lovely vista of the many small ponds in the very remote country to the southeast."

Jack chuckled; he had hiked enough to know the truth.

Actually, the tower may have been closed, but it was not impossible to climb. All you had to do was pull yourself up on the first landing (the first flight of stairs had been ripped out years ago). The rest was easy, though you had to be careful on a few of the steps, not step hard in the middle.

At the third landing, he cleared the treetops, and the wind came across the top of his head and blew away the deer flies that had been circling and jabbing at his ears. He stuck out his chin and dried his beard in the wind. As he climbed to the top of the tower on what had to be the clearest day of the year—maybe even of the decade—he realized the guidebook had been completely wrong, or one of those intervening mountains had quietly collapsed and left this unobstructed view sixty miles to the northeast, into the center of the Adirondack wilderness.

He was so excited he got cold chills.

Each new flight of weathered wooden steps revealed a new, more distant rank of mountains. First, the peaks just north of Piseco Lake, whose shapes he recognized from driving up that way, but whose names he did not know. They were shaped like alpine hats, covered with green velvet.

Then Snowy Mountain, at least twenty-five miles north, with its strange white cube shape on top—not snow, no, certainly not in August.

Beyond Snowy, as he climbed higher on the tower, the central High Peaks reared up like a single unit—Algonquin, Colden, Marcy, the one in the middle resembling a volcanic cone with a wisp of cloud above it. He thought, "I'd know that profile from any direction. When I'm eighty years old, they'll still line up just that way, even if the trees are gone and the Earth's climate has changed and something else is growing on those slopes. Or if we have another ice age, those mountains will stick up like that above the ice. The three of them." As if chilled by Jack's speculation of future glaciers, the air turned cold on the Hogback Mountain tower. The steel joints groaned as the wind blew down from the north, and Jack imagined it had passed over snowfields in the High Peaks.

To the southwest, he could make out the tiny pink roof of the Matterhorn, and in that context Sandy—and all her fury—diminished to the head of a pin.

"It's so small now," he yelled. "So small it doesn't mean a thing. Hear that, Sandy?"

He pulled himself up into the cabin at the top of the tower, six feet square, where a ranger used to look out over the Lost River wilderness in search of forest fires before the tower was decommissioned. Jack had come up here when he was a boy and talked to the ranger, an old man with a mustache. Everyone called him Buckskin, for reasons buried so deep in the past that even Buckskin had forgotten.

"I guess I have part Indian blood." The nameplate on his khaki shirt said his name was Eugene Roberson.

"Injuns used to live around here, didn't they?" the young boy asked.

"A few," the old man said. "More of them north of here. Did you know there was a Squaw mountain up that way?"

"Really?"

"Yup. They named it for my grandma, or my great grandma."

"They did? Where is it? Point it out, Buckskin."

"Oh, you can't see it today, too much haze. Maybe once every twenty years it clears enough." Then the old ranger told him about clear summers, and hazy ones, the woods catching fire all the way to Cathead Mountain and Three Ponds Mountain.

Jack remembered Buckskin telling him the names of the mountains close by, as he stood next to a round table that occupied the middle of the cabin, with a topographic map on top, and a straight metal bar that Buckskin held between his fingers and spun around on a center pin from which you could sight the mountains shown on the map. Jack would get down on the floor and put his eye to the pointer and think how each mountain drew closer to him that way. He always dreamed of mountains. He still did.

Buckskin's old table was still there, but the map and sighting bar had been taken out. The map had represented a radius of less than twenty miles from Hogback, and was irrelevant to the identification he was trying to make. Beyond the central High Peaks, he could make out an even more distant mountain, a shimmering blue pyramid—probably Whiteface, more than seventy miles away, where the alpine events would be held during the Olympics that winter.

He thought about skiing on Whiteface—"Greatest Vertical Drop in the East." It seemed as far away as Europe. There was a tourist attraction on the other side of the mountain, called the "North Pole," where his parents had taken him when he was a boy. It had a year-round Santa, elves, reindeer. He remembered the tall white pole covered with dry ice—touching it quickly with his bare hand. Another kid had tried to lick the pole, and his tongue had stuck, then someone held a candle under his tongue to free him.

He hoped the North Pole was still there, and it took on the force of a magnetic pole; he could feel the pull.

He wanted to strap on skis and head out into the central wilderness—northeast, across the enormous country of named and unnamed lakes and mountains that lay between. Seventy miles cross-country, if only it would snow and let him through. He thought, If I can get through all the way to Van Hoevenberg everything else in my life will be easy or won't matter. In August, in his head, he was already skiing.

On February 8th, 1980, Paul's snow chart read TWELVE
INCHES, and POWDER, MORE COMING!

Sandy and Paul ate breakfast at the Coffee Shop. In a few
minutes it would be nine o'clock, when Paul would walk over and
start the lifts at the Ski Bowl. He imagined lift lines, if the local
alcoholics got up out of bed and did what was right. His father was
one of them, he thought, as he named all the men who used to ski
the mountain but who now always had an excuse.

Paul hoped to get in a few hours of skiing himself now that conditions were perfect. He would have asked Jack to ski with him, but
Jack had disappeared, taken off on his cross-country skis the day
before, alone. One day Jack would go out alone and break a leg
twenty miles from the highway. He'd die in the woods and his body
never be found.

"I don't really mind," Sandy said. "It was like he didn't want to
be serious about anything. We were having another one of our
talks, and he just got up and said, 'It looks like good skiing. See ya.'
And that was that. He went off with a heavy pack on his back.
Took all his special food."

"He was right about the skiing," Paul said, squinting from the
snowlight coming through the south window. "Hey, I'll switch on
the lights for Edelweiss tonight. We'll have to walk up the slope,
but it'll be fun."

"Night skiing! When was the last time the Ski Bowl had night
skiing!"

"Never. We're not insured for it. We set it up, but we never had it,
because we're poor," he said. "You have to ski at your own risk."

"I could ski that trail blindfolded. God, what do I care about risk!"

Before going out to ski that night they watched the Six O'clock
News. Because of the Olympics, the weatherman did a special
report on snow cover in the Adirondacks. Lake Placid didn't have
more than a dusting. The map showed snow depths by color.
Yellow: only a trace up to two inches—an area including Lake
Placid (a shot of the main street of the village, totally devoid of
snow, people walking around looking puzzled and anxious). Light
orange: two to six inches—most of the Adirondacks, reaching to
within six miles of Lake Placid, including the area immediately

south of the Olympic cross-country trails at Mount Van Hoevenburg (there was a shot of workers spreading man-made snow on the trails, dump trucks lined up in the parking lot, full of snow). Red orange: six inches to a foot—an area extending through the central Adirondacks in a ski-able wedge pointing northeast, but not reaching where it was really needed. Dark Red: more than a foot—the Western Adirondacks.

"Looks like they should have held the Olympics down here," Sandy said, coughing and barking as she laughed.

"Wouldn't that be something. Where would they hold the downhill?"

The interesting thing was the Olympic Motel of Lost River was packed for the weekend, and the overflow had gone to the Matterhorn, into the bad rooms with the velvet paintings and crooked mirrors. One of the guests at the Olympic had brought out a guitar and sung at the Coffee Shop. Paul's father had taken out the fiddle for a duet, and Sandy had seen a tear run down Paul's cheek.

"I'm the one who should be crying, but I don't feel a thing," Sandy said. "If my life is falling apart, then why aren't I miserable?"

"I guess you like to be in a crowded room, with a maple fire, and a mug of cocoa in your hand." Paul was just saying this; his mind was on something else.

"I know where he is."

"Yeah, so do I."

But they did not discuss it further, and when they finished their cocoa, they carried their skis and poles to the Ski Bowl, where Paul turned on the lights, and they climbed Edelweiss. Sandy always looked straight ahead and broke the trail up the hill, but Paul stepped out of the pale elongated circle of light for a moment and looked out over the valley. To the northeast, he saw the familiar curve of the Lost River—if not the river itself, then the open marshland that formed its border.

No sign of a skier's headlamp fanning across a snowy meadow; nothing but a radio tower to the south, the red light rippling up and down. Sandy had stopped to catch her breath. She looked at him, she had something to say, but no breath to say it, and he looked away towards the village, where "Matter" flickered for a moment, and then went out.

THREE WINDOWS

Seven years Donna drove past Carol's store without stopping. Once or twice she'd slowed enough to notice the layout of the buildings. She saw a face in an upstairs window one time when she braked to avoid collision with a pickup truck coming out of the parking lot. Usually, she drove by quickly, worried they might see her in the car. But one day in January on her way back from Stowe, she decided she would stop for gas and take it from there. A complete stranger might come out to the gas pumps, or Carol, or it might be her husband Doug. Donna had barely known him at Potsdam; she didn't think he would recognize her, and perhaps her best friend wouldn't either.

North Bay, population fifty. It wasn't dark yet, but their Mobil sign was lit up. She put on the brakes and turned to enter the North Bay Supply Company parking lot ("D. and C. Borden, Proprietors"), freshly plowed as if they had figured she was coming. She didn't need gas; and their price, printed out child-like in large numerals on white cardboard above the two old-fashioned pumps, was ten cents more than she was used to paying. So she would go up on the porch and look at magazines for a minute, and then leave. There was a woman up there now, pear-shaped, taking down a magazine—who might be Carol, if Carol now weighed over two hundred pounds. The thought made her head ring.

She got out of the car and called out in a trembling voice, "Carol?"

"She's upstairs," the woman said without turning around.

Donna asked, "Is the store open? I just need cigarettes."

"Yep, they got 'em." The woman had a scarf over her mouth and her glasses were frosted over. She said in muffled fashion, "Just go in. When you open the door, a buzzer goes off and one of the family comes gallopin' downstairs."

The family—my God, how many *were* there?

Donna took hold of the doorknob. A sign said, "No bare feet." When Donna looked down at her boots, she saw an old shoe-brush nailed to the floor, but she didn't use it, because her boots were clean and the brush wasn't. She looked in the window—a Genesee beer sign flashed on and off, and there was no one in the store.

I may as well go ahead with it, make the buzzer go off, make somebody come down the stairs. She opened the door and walked in, didn't hear any buzzer, but almost immediately a pair of heavy feet came tromping down the stairs—a man or a woman?

"Hi," Carol said blandly, as if greeting an ordinary customer. Then she recognized Donna and hugged her, which vaguely irritated Donna because she didn't think she would be recognizable. While they hugged, Donna looked over Carol's shoulder at the store shelves—the tacky gifts and souvenirs, the fishing tackle, the canned goods for . . . the desperate thief in the night. Did they lock the door? Carol was asking her questions about the past ten years of her life, and Donna was saying, "Calm down, calm down. We'll get to that eventually . . . . In fact, if you have a cabin available, I guess I'll spend the night." Carol wore a green wool scarf over her hair; she had gained just enough weight to make Donna feel comfortable about staying.

Carol clapped her mittens and said in a familiar way, "Oh, that's great. That's just great. I can't believe we're standing here together. So much to talk about."

"One thing though," Donna said. "I wonder if there's a pay phone around here. I need to make a call real quick."

Carol waved her arm: "Out in front along the highway. But if you stay out there long, you'll freeze, so make it quick, kid, and come right upstairs for beef stew."

Carol waited for a while, and then went to her bedroom window, to gaze out over the parking lot that Doug had so neatly plowed, where she could see only two cars—an old brown Chevy Nova—Kathy Shink's car (still down there on the porch; she came here to escape from her husband, never bought anything)—and Donna's, a low-slung sportscar that seemed inappropriate for winter driving. She would have to find out what Donna did for a living. She was so thin!

She could see Donna gesturing in the phone booth, moving around as much as the small space allowed. She was probably talking with her husband, if she still had one. Or somebody who could make her hang her head back so that she was looking straight up, then clutch at her neck, then swing around suddenly, then pound her fist on the glass. Careful, girl, don't crack it or we'll have to pay the phone company.

Donna filled the booth with hot air, and a circle of condensation began to grow, hiding her head from Carol's view. Carol thought, "She's going to fog up the glass and then disappear. She's not real."

Holly started to clear the table. "No honey, not yet. Wipe off where Dad was sitting and put on a clean place-setting. We've got company."

When Donna eventually came upstairs, Carol would talk about how the picture window was steamed up so much you couldn't look out at the lake, the best feature of the living room (She didn't want Donna to look at the pathetic furniture, left-over from what her mother had not sold when she closed down the North Bay Sunset Motel). But the view was special—the lake glowed at night in the winter, almost as though it were lit from below.

Doug had said something like that, in one of his more poetic moments. The image would appeal to Donna. Carol would try to wake up Doug, though she wasn't sure what he'd make of Donna. He was conked out on the floor in front of the television, and the three-year-old, Christopher, lay on his father's stomach, watching cartoon figures flit silently across the screen. Doug liked to have him there—said it helped him digest supper! Carol supposed that her younger daughter Jodi was in her bedroom playing the toy xylophone. Maybe the noise came from the TV. This apparent domestic perfection was not something she had arranged for the random day when Donna would drop in, although she felt glad that her own life was peaceful, and that she had nothing to hide. The consequence of almost total isolation from other people. Sure, there were other people around, but her husband and her children were the only ones she could possibly care for.

They had recently winterized their cabins, and rented out the best to a young couple, kids just out of high school. What was the boy's name? Bruce or Brad. She didn't see much of him, since he worked for the town highway department and got up early in the morning to plow and sand. He swore a lot. The girl she knew better; Julie was pregnant and slept late most mornings, dragging over to the store around noon to buy one or two items, like potato chips and cat food, and they'd talk for a while. Brad and Julie kept an account going, paid up every couple of weeks, which was about as reliable as one could expect from the year-round people. For that, and for other reasons, Carol had given them a Swifts turkey out of the freezer case at Christmas, left over from when nobody had bought any for Thanksgiving. She knew the boy drank a good part of his pay, and she thought the girl looked terribly thin for being seven months pregnant. Well, Carol could say she had provided them with a good cabin and turkey to get them through the next month.

Donna would sleep in the other cabin, closer to the lake. It was clean; no one had stayed in Shoreview since October, and she had vacuumed afterward. When the children were in bed, the two women could sit down and talk. Maybe Doug would go to bed early. Carol stood in her kitchen and wondered what had finally caused Donna to come to North Bay; maybe Donna was lonely. She went back to her bedroom window, where Holly stood in the dark, watching Donna in the phone booth.

"What are you doing, honey?"

"Mommy, that lady, she's been in the phone booth for a long time. She keeps putting in more change." She giggled nervously.

Doug got up. "Hey, I almost forgot I had to go out and check the Coopers' furnace. Should have done it hours ago. They're probably sitting there freezing."

"Did you check everything else on the board, honey? I took a couple of calls while you were asleep."

Doug asked, "Any emergencies?"

She put her hand on his back. "I don't think so. Also, Donna is here. You know, Donna Witbeck."

The name didn't register, and Doug put on his ski cap and went out.

"Who is Donna Witbeck?" Holly asked.

Carol went downstairs when she heard the buzzer go off. Donna was smoking in the store.

"Down to my last cigarette," she said, strumming the counter. "I'm wondering whether you have my brand."

"Salems?"

"No. Players."

Later, Donna smoked in her cabin, and smiled at the funny ashtray. It was a flattened swan. The neck formed a silly handle that she tapped with her little finger. Where'd this stuff *come* from, anyway—garage sales? The vase on the table might be worth a few dollars, even though it was ugly, the worst shade of green with pink flowers writhing about. On the knotty-pine wall was a carved-moose horror, a kind of bas-relief in wood, painted in blue and orange. Unbelievable. She puffed smoke at the moose to scare it away.

She liked the fireplace, its crude unmatched stones, and the warm raised hearth where she sat in her robe trying to wind down from the conversation. She had survived, and considered survival a major accomplishment. It had been hard to talk without a cigarette (sold downstairs, forbidden upstairs). She hadn't said much anyway, mostly "Uh-huh." Carol, on the other hand, could not stop talking about friends from college. It wasn't all positive, so Donna paid attention.

Then Carol started to tell stories about the people who lived along Silver Lake and the woods nearby, all fifty of them. Donna couldn't keep the first names straight—mostly from one family. Evidently, ninety percent were on welfare, and those who were married were cheating on each other quite openly. These facts seemed a healthy antidote to what she had seen earlier down in the store—a Community Calendar, in which birthdays and anniversaries were noted for every citizen of North Bay and its neighboring town, South Kilns. The month of January was nearly barren, and Donna remembered all three names: Mildred LeGow, Harold Shink, and Christopher Borden (circled in green, Carol's little boy). One anniversary: Debby and Glenn Stanger, with "first" in parentheses. Who would get married in January? When she found Carol and Doug's June anniversary ("tenth"), with stylized hearts and roses above—"The Bordens"—she turned away quickly.

The lake was important. All kinds of facts about the lake—how deep, how acidic. Eight miles long. If you could only see it. Well, where the hell was it? Donna wasn't sure which direction to look.

Everything outside looked white, or what she perceived as white in almost total darkness. She went to her bedroom window and turned off the light. No more than fifty feet away was the broad, blue-white expanse of the lake, scarred like the moon's surface with snowmobile trails. All right, now that she finally had a view of it, she had to admit she was impressed, or frightened. On the other side of the lake, she could see four or five lights—maybe street-lights, since they were evenly spaced. She saw the headlights of a single car slowly maneuver along the shore, then disappear behind an island, then return to view.

A local was driving home from a bar, very carefully. The people up here had their bars, and that was about *all* they had for enter-tainment. Two or three of the bars stayed open in winter. She had seen a bar not more than a couple of miles down the road from North Bay, with Christmas lights strung along the eaves in primary colors that shook her to her very bones, and a Genesee sign glow-ing in the window. The locals drank Genesee. The Bordens had it stacked six-feet high in the middle of the store, on special, and no imported beers except Molsons.

She thought back to the bar with the Christmas lights. There had been no more than four cars in the parking lot. She was trying to think of the details—the name of the place had been . . . the Lost River Inn. That name had panicked her, and then a flashing light put her at ease: "We are Open." It gave her a warm feeling, then and now—the fact that space had been plowed and cars were able to pull up close.

But she'd never go in one of those bars, no matter how lonely or lost. Not that she wouldn't go in *any* bar, but she preferred a dif-ferent type.

She began to hear a buzzing sound like a chainsaw, and saw a pair of headlights where she thought the lake was. The headlights moved at different speeds. What was wrong with her eyesight? Then she saw the two lights separate, and realized that each was a headlight for an individual snowmobile. One of the lights slowed down, and the snowmobile came up the embankment, stopping very close to her window. It let out a puff of blue smoke as the driver cut the engine.

So that's her husband, the man pushing the snowmobile into the shed. Where has he been? I wonder. Do I have any right to know?

The man gave Donna's cabin a look. Maybe he noticed her silhouette. She moved away from the window and tightened the knot on her robe.

She put out her cigarette on the swan.

In bed, she looked at very old magazines, dating from the seventies. The advice they gave still seemed to apply.

"Who is this Donna Witbeck?" Doug asked at midnight, getting into bed with Carol. He had beer breath.

"Oh come on, honey, I was asleep. I'll tell you in the morning."

"I'm sleeping late."

"All right," she said. "When you get up, you can make French toast, and we'll look out over the first reflection of sunlight on the lake, and I'll tell you everything."

"I know you will."

"But before we talk," she said, "we better put the girls on the schoolbus. Holly has been paying close attention to everything. She doesn't miss a thing."

They slept peacefully. It did not snow again, and no one called in the middle of the night needing help.

Donna woke up at first light with a sore throat, the kind where the irritation seemed to stretch to the very corners of her eyes. She heard someone gunning his engine, an engine with no muffler, and then the hard slap of a flimsy door slamming in the next cabin.

God, it must be ten degrees below zero! Ice *inside* the window. Damn, where did I put the cigarettes?

She went in the bathroom and brushed her teeth in the ice water, yipping when she touched the cold faucet handle. What the heck, they offered me the couch and I didn't take it. I have only myself to blame—for the fact that I couldn't stay up all night to keep the fire going.

She looked over at the main building.

Long blue icicles, almost thick enough to be pillars, stretched from the second-story eaves to the ground—making an ice palace, it seemed, particularly in this early morning light. Under the layers of ice glowed an odd pink clapboarding, several planks swelling out as if diseased.

The first floor had no windows on this side, but several shed-like appendages, one with a crudely painted sign—"OIL CANS." The words were actually in quotes, as if the objects they referred to as "oil cans" might turn out to be something else. She focused on those words. As clumsily painted as they were, and in spite of the dumb quotation marks, they meant something definite. One could break the ice, open that door, and find oil cans, probably different types in different colors arranged on several shelves. She thought that if she went out, broke the ice, opened the door, and found something else—like a pair of shoes she had lost at college—then she would probably go into a coma. She touched her neck, and felt how the dull pain there was connected to the more acute pain in her throat.

Closer towards the front end of the store she saw a bulkhead for the cellar. Other things down there I shouldn't wonder about.

Then, on the second floor, three tall windows, trimmed in dark green. In one window hung a piece of artwork a child must have made out of construction paper, a wintry fir tree, three triangular branches on both left and right, more or less representing what was real outside. Another window had the shade down and a "tot-finder" decal on the glass, information for the firemen when this place burned, as it would one day, Donna thought with a slight degree of comfort. The North Bay Supply Company could burn to the ground a week from now, and I won't even hear about it.

The third window suddenly lit up and she flinched.

There she saw Carol standing naked in front of a mirror, work-ing on her long blonde hair, what had been tied up in a scarf the day before—taking it out of a towel, drying it with the towel, then shaking it. Leaning in various directions to make it hang loose and dry. Then brushing it.

She was thin! Not anorexic, but certainly not one pound overweight. That extra weight had been her clothes, her long underwear and turtleneck and vest.

One of the little girls came into the frame, and Carol began brushing the girl's hair. They looked at each other together in the mirror. Donna wondered whether they could see her. Of course not—too much of themselves to monopolize their attention.

When Donna drove away in her car a few minutes later, before the store opened, she thought about how she had spared them her throat infection. Or she hoped she had. Would they all come down sick the next day and blame her? And she sensed that if she had stayed any longer, she would have learned all was not well; or would have sown the necessary seed of disorder in some fertile patch of their lives. That fertile patch in other lives had never been hard for Donna to find.

Knowing the risk of opening the wrong door or looking in the wrong window, she drove away without saying good-bye and preserved her concept of the Borden family as a counterbalance to the details of her own life.

When she drove out of North Bay ("Cedar Lake, 14"), she made the lake disappear from view like a page in a magazine, and on the next page, she saw a person in a yard next to a small shack, chopping wood. It looked like the woman from the store porch who had been reading Ladies Home Journal. A man was tossing logs at her, and she was handling them as if they did this every day. Donna stepped on the accelerator.

HEMLOCKS

White pine growing back, almost like it never been logged. Hemlocks the same, as if never cut. Weaving together in thick dark green. There's one stretch of the hemlock out toward Kilkenny, I know of it from my rambling in the woods every day. Never been cut or burnt over. You'd think they woulda cleared it out and built a tannery up there, but I guess they didn't have the water up there on the plateau.

The past twenty years that's all I do. Pick up things. Check the trees. Some real beauties out there. White pine. I know the way. Not the way the snowmobiles take, but another way that's been walked for two hundred years.

You sometimes find a considerable portion of wild land nobody never crossed, and it could be your footprints are the first, even the Indians didn't make a path over this land. You take a piece of paper and you draw ten points along the edge of that piece of paper, connect them this way and that. Oftentimes, you leave a blank place on the paper after all them lines are crossed, a place that's not on the trail to noplace. That's what I'm talking about. And where I'm going today.

I ain't going from no place to no place, so I go into blank space, never logged. Somehow, I find my way around.

I'm looking for the man that raised me three years after Mom and Dad died, Luke Willis, the old hermit of Harristown.

You take a look at the pictures Edna has over at the post office, some of them *real* old. I 'member there was a big one in a frame of old Luke when he come down to Sewall's store that's now a pile of worthless lumber and broken pieces of brick, quarter mile below where the Mohican Hotel was, when he come down to trade there. It was 1910, I think. I mean when the picture got took for Harper's magazine. Luke and his squaw lady, Theresa. They had that picture in a frame hanging up on the wall of the post office many years. Famous, but I forgot why. They cut it out of Harper's magazine. I don't know where they got it now.

Luke had a white beard came all the way down to his waist. He wore a beaver hat and a raccoon vest, leather breeches. The lady dressed like a white woman. He was sixty then, by his own counting. No one knew where or when he was borned. Luke didn't know. He told me what he thought was true, what his ma told him, and so forth, but I don't bother to tell no one else since they already say, "Don't talk to Armand Shink, he's crazy, shoulda gone into the county home a long time ago." They still come up from Tannersburgh and ask for me. They're ready to give me a ride down there the next time they see me, but they won't see me.

I never ran into Luke after that picture was took, I mean, I was playing ball somewhere, living in cheap hotel rooms in another part of the country. And when I come back everything's all changed. Fire and water. Fire and water and wind. I gotta learn my trails all over again.

And so when I come back to Lost River at the end of my ball career, there's one place I gotta go first, because I think old Luke might still be alive. 1930, it was.

I got this place on the trail to Harristown, used to be a logging road, where it goes over a rock outcrop and passes the old foundation for what everybody called the old Shink place (my name), the one that burned down before I was born, I don't know if my mom and dad lived there. Nobody knows.

I got this place I can look out over the valley, and it was years ago, years ago, even before the judge took off with all that gold and certificates, why we're all so poor. I'm walking to Harristown, not to see old Luke, because by then I know he must be gone, but the shanty might be there, I just want to check.

It woulda been years since I walked up there. I don't keep track. There was a rocky outcrop facing south over the great valley of the Elk River, so as you could see that open place they called the Great Vly, out towards Tannersburgh. Fifty-mile view up there. Catskill mountains peeking over the last ridge you could see, three bumps. I used to sit there and watch the hawks swooping up the hillside. And I don't think there's no hawks around hereabouts no more.

And I could see the little farms out there before you got to the Vly, with the hedgerows between them, some dairy cattle moving about. Yep, they used to have farms back then.

So I was coming up on the overlook. Passed a cairn with four rocks I set up so I'd know when to stop. Turned around to look at the view and almost fell off the cliff. It's like an ocean out there, past the first two ridges, the reservoir starting to fill up to the rim they established for it and where they burnt and dragged out most of the trees, bright blue water, not to its level it has today. What I mean is you could still see the last bits, the high parts of some little town they haven't torn down all the way, East Williston I think it was. I used to ride down there on horseback and court a girl. Never married her. I used to catch a train down there but they pulled up the tracks to use the iron in the War.

I came up on a slope that was covered with hemlock, new growth. They don't cut hemlock here no more. And it's coming back. They don't even thin it out, so you have to walk around the hemlock stands, and you come into one of those blank areas, *real* wilderness, almost surrounded by how the Lost River curls around, flowing north, then east, then south towards Buttermilk Falls and such.

It used to be I could look down from that height of land— upstream, not off the other way where the goddamn reservoir is, and I'd see the smoke coming up from Luke's fire, find his place thataway. Nothing doing this time. The wind blows the wrong way. So I gotta walk up alongside the Lost River clambering over a mess of boulders. I'm a forty-year-old man back then. Not fat. Never smoked, chewed some when I could afford it and find a place to buy it.

Wished I'd had a knife with me, a saw would be even better, when I have to work my way around the rapids, because the woods is like a jungle.

It's a five mile hike without the twists and turns and running around in circles. I just take a loaf of white bread in my knapsack what I picked up from the day-old rack at Edna's. But I know what else to eat and what not to. The things that you can make a sandwich out of when you're out in the woods.

Midway up Golden Creek is where Eugene Roberson used to have his hunting camp, on a ledge sticking out over the third rapids. It was just Gene and Luke up this way. Gene and Luke never spoke one to the other as long as I knew them, Gene was the younger man, and when the State put the tower on Hogback Mountain, they wanted *him* to be the fire observer. That was during the years I was away, while I was losing track of my friend Luke. Luke knew the woods better, but Gene was the perfect man when they needed somebody to go up on a mountain and watch for fires. Good eyes, bad temper. We never missed him when he was up there on the mountain. We used to call him the Owl back in those days. People would say, "The old Owl is up on the mountain," that's what they'd say, and shake their head and smile.

Anyways, old Gene Roberson cleared out from his old camp on Golden Creek because they set him up in a regular cabin with a roof on Hogback Mountain. It's still up there. Winters, he'd stay with his niece down in Schenectady.

The pine woods takes over as you go up the valley. It's fairly level, no steep banks, and there's nice clean swimming in the pools the creek forms here and there. I know it from when I was a boy. I mean that's where I was raised for three years, no school or nothing.

Armand sees a smoke haze in the great hemlock forest.

What the hell. He never swore out loud.

If I don't turn around and walk fast I could turn into a dandy pile of potash.

His nose still works—it can tell what type of wood is burning. And this ain't no wood smoke. It's wet leaves burning.

We're a long way from the town dump, he thinks. I figure it would be the Harristown dump if they got any. Wind's blowing from the Northeast.

Some goddamn smoke signal!

When I'm about ready to be taken into the sky, the old hermit had told him, I make a bed of leaves and set them on fire. Winter, it's pine boughs. White pine. Can't get hemlock.

Summer, it's maple, beech, and others.

What do you mean, can't get hemlock? Look around, you old fool!

I wanna know how long this smoke been hanging in these here woods. Roberson call it in yet, I wonder. Old man Roberson, he's crippled and deaf anyway, can't barely climb down from the tower, need a younger man up there. I coulda done it. Wouldn't even need a map.

COVERED BRIDGE

In early summer 1930 the two boys went down Burdick Road to the north branch of Elk River, down by the covered bridge where they always fished, and measured with their eyes the new water-line. It had rained for a week, a foot of rain, and the bridge was now more of a boat than a bridge. Its iron replacement spanned the creek a few hundred yards upstream, and you could stand under the new bridge and look up at the cars as they went over. You could throw rocks up through the iron grid if they were small enough and see if you could hit somebody's gas tank. And if you did, and they got mad and stopped, there were plenty of good places to hide.

When the reservoir reached its high water level later that year, it was supposed to drown all the land up to the base of the Falls.

The largest part of the town had been downstream from the bridge, and everyone from that part had moved out, leaving empty husks of house, church, barn, as well as various cats and dogs that ran up into the woods and turned wild. From the bridge you could see just the steeple of the de-consecrated East Williston Methodist Church, from which someone had removed the cross a month ago, though they took a chance on getting stuck and sinking into the mud, and there was no guarantee they'd be rescued just because they were holding up a cross.

The hymn-board with the hymn numbers still on it and a few odd hymnals washed ashore one day. That's what the boys found the last time they came down here.

For the month of April, every able-bodied man in town had been employed by the Hudson River Black River Regulating Board, which paid them to dig up the bodies of their ancestors from the East Williston cemetery and move them up to the new cemetery on

Diamond Hill. This was a major task: since the closing of the tan-
neries at the beginning of the century, the cemetery population had
always outnumbered the living.

Those who still went to church had to travel twelve miles to
Tannersburgh. Not many did. They simply gave up church-going.
East Williston Methodist never did support their own preacher.
They were always on the circuit with Elk River Falls and Hawkin-
town and Rustic Bridge. Fifty people would show up for church
sometimes, back when they could get to it. The last time they went
to church, the people had to cross the water on a makeshift board-
walk that was nailed onto the porch of the church, and some of the
old folks wouldn't go but stood there on the embankment and cried
the whole time, saying how it had been bad luck to move the
bodies. And some boys misbehaved after service, went swimming
in their good clothes and caught a chill. Maybe they never needed
their good clothes after that Sunday, the last Sunday service ever at
East Williston Methodist. Then it rained and the water came up
faster than they had predicted and soaked the hymnals before they
could get them all.

It was Sunday morning in August, and the two boys went out on
the covered bridge to feel the rising water lift the bridge from its
stone piers. Johnny Shink and Larry Becker were both twelve.
They jumped out on the ruined bridge, over a new channel of water
that already washed over the old Diamond Hill road.

One, two, three, four . . .

Nine more to the golden door . . .

What's next . . .

I can't think of it, Johnny said.

I thought you knowed it.

Sometimes I do, sometimes I don't. My ma knows it, all that
kind of stuff.

Where'd it come from? Larry asked.

Just something we say. There used to be more to it, but my ma
doesn't say the rest of it anymore.

The boys pretended to fish, projecting long poles between the
vertical boards of the bridge. Fishing had been lousy all year. They
told each other they'd start going up to Lost River next year if they
could get rides.

My ma's sick today, Johnny said, tapping on old wood that smelled like cinnamon, the inside ribs of the covered bridge, the dying animal that groaned as the water lifted it.

I don't think this thing is nailed down real good, Larry said.

It *aint* nailed down. The bridge is sick, Johnny said. It's sick just like a person. Smells sick. All the fish are dead.

Nobody said anything for a while and you could just hear tapping or wood starting to break.

Your ma's always sick. She's a loony. Your daddy's always sick. He's a loony.

Daddy's got bad dreams, Johnny said, breaking off a piece of wood so he could look out at the reservoir. He pushed the wood through the hole he had made..

How do you know?

You know, Larry . . . you know back when your daddy and my daddy went down to East Williston to move those bodies from the graveyard?

Yep. They got five dollars for each body they dug up. More money than my pa made all year doing other work. We're rich now. What about it?

My daddy ain't been right since then. He can't work no more. He's spooked.

I know it. I seen him walkin out by the road.

You better get away from my daddy, Larry. Everything looks like a monster to him and he wants to kill it. My ma had to hide the shotgun on him.

Why's that?

'Cause he wanted to shoot her with it, that's why.

No, I wanna know why does he want to kill everything.

He never told us.

What about you?

What *about* me.

He ever point that shotgun at you, Johnny?

Nope. Just my ma. She makes him drop it. She looks at him funny and his hands open up. Like this (he dropped a stick of wood). He almost faints dead on the floor. I wish I could do that to him. He likes to break into my room and yell at me real late at night. I wish I could stop him like that. My eyes would light up in the dark and I'd make him drop dead right on the floor!

The boys aren't really fishing, just visiting. They stop talking when they hear a large board snap like a gun firing, and they leap from the bridge to the shore just as the bridge breaks loose and starts turning in a circle as if to accommodate a boat passing through with a tall mast.

Hey Johnny, are they just gonna *let* that bridge float away?

Looks like it. I don't see nobody around to haul it in.

You could build a new house out of that wood.

I know, it looks better than the wood on our house. They're just gonna let it sink out there.

Larry says, your house sinking, too?

Nope, just falling in t'wards the middle.

HAMILTON LAKE

Larry Becker's father had dropped so far out of sight and mind that when the Hamilton Lake people said "Larry," they didn't have to distinguish between Junior and Senior any more. They could refer to the old man as the "late Larry Becker," or better yet, "the *previous* Larry Becker," or save themselves the trouble and not refer to him at all. The old man sat entombed in the house all day, arthritis in his hands, his back bent in the middle almost at a ninety degree angle so that the easiest thing for him to do was stare at his shoes, and think, "Did I lace them right? Is there a hole on the bottom?" He could dress himself and put food in his mouth without dumping it on his lap more than half the time. But his son often wondered, why go on eating?

The old man had been a great craftsman when the hands were still good and the back was straight. He had designed and built a couple of the finest camps on Hamilton Lake. Larry wanted to have a real talk with him, ask his opinion about what to do with Mrs. Coover's porch, the chimney on Poplar Lodge, the boathouse on the Point—Larry made his living as a caretaker and handyman on the Lake.

But talking to the old man was like talking to a piece of furniture; he barely nodded his head, shook his knees, shivering even when the heat was turned up to eighty. Larry sometimes thought, I could turn it down to fifty.

Although he looked eighty, the old man was sixty-eight. His wife was dead, and Larry's twin sister Sharon lived at the Home for Adults down in Algonquin County, a few miles outside Tannersburgh. Winter time, Larry Jr. didn't get down there much, except Christmas, and now it was January and he had six more roofs to shovel before he went to bed that night. Larry wasn't thinking so much about family as he was about those twelve inches of snow soaking up the rain, gaining weight, threatening to collapse the roofs his father had built.

"Bye, Dad, gotta go to work." His Dodge pickup had a metal cap over the back to cover his tools and his gas cans. He always kept five gallons of gasoline just in case. You couldn't stand up under the cap, but you could sleep there with the tools if you got stranded somewhere, though in the winter you might wake up dead. "Wake up dead" was exactly the way he worded it in his mind, since he believed he would wake up a few hours after dying, and his life was nothing but a bad dream. In the *next* life, maybe he'd have a wife, a real house, kids, and such.

Now it was just raining and the roads weren't so bad except where the Town had plowed and his tires didn't have anything to catch on until they slid for a few feet and then bit down on some old crust of snow. He switched on the radio in the truck. He could just barely get WGY down in Schenectady, a phone-in show about nutrition. One crackpot was explaining to another how people got "red necks" from drinking frozen concentrated orange juice. About all he could get out of it. His neck itched from the collar of his wool shirt—that's where he got *his* red neck; he never drank any kind of orange juice. If he ever had breakfast, it was coffee. He switched to the CB for a while, and listened to Mickey Sue Quinn trying to make contact with Chuck Norland.

"Give up, lady," Larry said to himself. "Just give up." Then he thought, "Maybe she's alone. Chuck's out."

Mickey ran the Balsam Inn, a place to get fueled up, listen to other people talk, though not to talk yourself, so you had to watch how much you drank. Larry never had more than two, and he was satisfied no one had ever found out what was on his mind.

The Balsam was one of the few local bars that stayed open past Christmas. The Cook family used to own it. When Larry was a boy, Mr. Cook had played Santa at Christmas time, and Larry remembered sitting on his knee, asking for things. Years ago, people stayed at the Inn and skied at the old Mystic Mountain area, but the ski area had closed, and the Balsam was just a bar now, with sandwiches if you could talk Mickey into making them. Sometimes you'd see Chuck Norland behind the bar. More often, he was simply "out" or "upstairs" and Larry could tell from Mickey's tone of voice how quickly he had better start talking about the weather. Chuck was as big as a bear, heavily tattooed, a one-time lumberjack with International Paper over in Cedar Lake.

Chuck Norland's relationship with Mickey Quinn was not a topic you'd bring up, but something where you'd put two and two together and just nod your head. When people at the Balsam saw Larry sitting there nodding over his beer, not saying anything, generally he was putting two and two together.

In addition to running the Balsam, Mickey was the town clerk and treasurer for the fire department. She was a nice-looking woman for being over forty, a bit heavy. Her people lived over in Williston, where her father was the school-bus driver, still going at seventy. Mickey had inherited the Balsam after her first husband died. And now Chuck stayed there and kept the place up, to a degree. It was more like, he kept law and order, because most people were afraid of the man. He didn't have to say a word or move a muscle. People just assumed—maybe it was Mickey's occasional fat lip or arm bruise—that the man had a violent streak.

Mickey didn't have much on her mind as she moved around in the bar doing inventory. She had an intercom to listen to what was going on with the kids upstairs, and the intercom was hooked up to the Plectron in case there were any fire calls. Chuck had come back from the store and was working outside, removing charred two-by-fours from when the toolshed had burned. You could hear the thump of a heavy mallet, the shriek of nails coming out of the boards. He was good at tearing things down—and leaving the debris all over the yard—but never showed an inclination to build anything. There was plenty of building to do if he ever took a mind to it.

What were those shrieks from the squawk box? It wasn't the nails, but one of the kids upstairs misbehaving and the other reacting to it, as if they knew the sound would get her attention. Tommy was pulling Lisa's hair—that would do it.

She pressed the button. "All right Tommy, that's enough. You know I heard that."

"What? We're not doing nothing."

"Oh? I thought you were watching the TV."

"We're eating."

"Are you getting into those Fritos?"

She looked out the window at the headlights of a pickup truck parking out front.

"What did you say, Mom?"

"I said you were eating garbage."

"No we're not."

"Okay," she said. "Put the garbage away. I'm coming up in a minute, so there better not be no mess, you hear?"

Larry Becker came in the front door, looking worse than she'd ever seen him. He kind of dropped like a wet dog into his usual seat. No hat. Thick blond hair soaking wet, no beard or mustache. Mickey wanted to wipe his face with a napkin. She got out a cold Genny Creme Ale and a chilled glass. She turned up the thermostat. To start a conversation, she nodded toward the squawk box.

"Just tell me those kids are staying out of trouble. If you can convince me they're not tearing up my living room, then I don't have to traipse up there and see what I don't want to see."

"Sounds like someone's hammering something."

"That's Chuck," she said brightly. "Trying to take down the rest of the back shed that burnt last week."

"Oh yeah, that one." Larry had been there with the rest of the guys to put out the fire. She hoped he realized how grateful she was, but Larry wouldn't even let her mention it. He waved his hand to change the subject.

She said, "So how's your dad?"

"Oh, about the same." Another wave of the hand. "Chuck need any help back there?"

"Larry, you sit still," she said, almost reaching over to hold him. "He likes doing that. I'm glad he's happy today, so let's not spoil his party. You know what I mean?" Larry nodded. He knew.

The hammering stopped and Mickey flinched slightly. You could hear the TV going over the squawk box, a game show with regular bursts of cheering.

"You out working tonight, Larry?" You had to keep asking questions to get any conversation out of him.

"Yep. 'Fraid so." She opened up another Genny for him. This one she wouldn't write down on his tab.

Now what would he be doing on this miserable night—what kind of work? Home couldn't be much of a comfort for him, but at least it was warm, she thought. You sometimes wondered whether any-

one lived out there in that awful shack on Pinnacle Road, no other
houses nearby, just the burnt-out shell of the old Pinnacle Bar, and
then you'd see the one little window facing the road with an orange
lampshade lit up. That was Larry's. Beyond the lampshade, she had
no idea what lay inside. Evidently, places to sit and sleep and eat.
And probably not much else. Indoor plumbing? Did anyone ever
go in and clean? Did Larry do laundry? He didn't smell bad; he
smelled like maple smoke. Maybe he took showers and did his
laundry in the places he took care of.

Larry took out a cigarette, reached into his jacket and pulled out
a box of kitchen matches.

"We have *book* matches, Larry," she said calmly. "Got our name
on them. Take as many as you like." She dumped out a jar of book
matches on the counter.

He nodded as he lit up with a kitchen match. She had forgotten
he smoked. Mickey used to smoke until Chuck made her quit.

"So," Larry said as he finished his cigarette. "My first job's at
Coover's place. Roof needs to be cleared off. I gotta hustle out 'cause
I don't get paid for letting people's roofs collapse, you know."

"I know. Just a minute, Larry. I gotta talk with upstairs."

She pushed the talk button.

"Tommy, turn off that damn TV."

"What?"

"Turn it off. Is Chuck up there?" She grabbed Larry's arm and held
tight. He looked at her and smiled, as if he thought she were making
some kind of pass at him, but that wasn't what she meant by it—at
least for now. "Don't leave yet, Larry. Do you want some cocoa?
Tommy, if Chuck is up there, in the bathroom, in the kitchen, you
tell him to get his ass down here right now." She turned to Larry.
"Chuck's not that busy. Every day I have to find work to get him off
his butt. Otherwise, he hangs around and drinks up the profits."

Larry stood up, nervous to get going.

"Mom, he's not up here. Mom, I'm hungry."

"I'll be up in a moment."

"Bye Mickey," Larry mumbled. She watched him go out the
front door and told herself if she had any sense at all, she'd get rid
of old Chuck and ask Larry to come live at the Balsam. For one
thing, he was better looking. They could smoke together. And he
was a genuine handyman, who could shore up the roof, do the elec-

trical, the plumbing. The yardwork. Carry out all the junk that had piled up over the past four years—the dead refrigerators, chainsaws, lawn mowers, broken bicycles, cash registers. All Chuck ever said was, "Hey, that stuff might be worth something. You'll get good money for that stuff if you wait long enough."

And she said, "If you think it's worth something, honey, then you buy it from me." That shut him up good, because Chuck never had any money to back up his statements; all he had was what she paid him.

Larry looked at the side mirror as he drove away from the Balsam and saw Mickey out on the porch waving at him. Did she want to be nice to him, or did she want him to rehabilitate Chuck? Did she want to go to bed with him? Where would they do it? He just kept driving. No way was he going to have that guy working with him. Everyone knew he was a firebug. It was all over Hamilton Lake. You'd turn your back on Chuck and the next thing you knew your pants were on fire. The main problem was, nobody had ever caught him in the act.

The road to Poplar Point took him over a high open meadow where he could look out toward the lake and see the island. He wouldn't be able to take the snow machine out to the island today, what with all the rain and warm weather. And so the McAllister place was out of reach, but wouldn't collapse since the roof was steep. He thought of April 1980 when the back wing burned: the lake was clear of ice and the firemen took the pumper boat out from the Point and saved the rest of the place, the main part that Larry's father had built. And his father had been well enough to talk with him about it. It was the last time they had talked.

Larry remembered an odd thing—seeing Chuck Norland sitting out there in his boat in Little Bay, watching the fire as if it had been something on TV. Bad back or something, Mickey said later. Larry didn't have to ask the question before she answered it. She knew Chuck had been out there not helping.

The lights were twinkling at nine or ten different places along the lakeshore, and each point of light worked at his heart in an odd way; he shook it off. Then it came back—kind of gnawed at him when he thought how everybody took things for granted.

Larry maneuvered his pick-up slowly down along Dexter Road,

and passed the Buckley place, where the people kept the heat and lights on all winter, and the attic got so warm the snow slid off on metal slides. Rich people. Larry had taken care of the place when it was first built, but now that the Buckleys had family members coming in and out so much all year, they didn't need him anymore. It wasn't one of his dad's camps, anyway. It looked newfangled, almost like a house built in a factory, or something in California he had seen in a magazine. They had put it up on the foundation of the old Mohican Hotel that burned thirty years ago, even before Larry was born. Dad fought that fire, with a bunch of other old guys who were all dead now, except Johnny Shink, who was seventy and still the fire chief. Larry thought about an ancient picture on the wall down at the firehouse—of Dad and Johnny Shink and the rest of them sitting on the big front porch of the Mohican, squinting because of the sun.

What if they had another fire there? It wasn't his brain that raised the question, but the same force that gnawed at his heart, that told him he'd lost out compared to other people. It went away after a while.

Now he could see the old gray canoe-paddle sign for Mrs. Coover's place, so he pulled over. He already had a ladder set up against the roof from the last time he shoveled it. When the Coovers came back in late April, he'd have to ask the old lady whether she wanted him to do the porch roof—new shingles, new plywood, or tear the whole blame thing down. Put up a deck like some of the modern places. When he shoveled the roof he wouldn't dare step on it, but he worked from the top of the ladder with a long-handled hoe, raking the snow methodically. Sometimes he'd think, "This is a pan of vanilla fudge. I'll cut off this piece, and eat it . . . ." That kept him going for a while. He couldn't get every flake, but the main bulk of the snow came off okay. If the porch collapsed, it would prove his point, though they might get mad at him and hire Harold Shink to do all their work for them.

That's okay. Larry would kill Chuck Norland somehow and go live with Mickey. Somehow, he'd get rid of the man.

He worked by the light from his pick-up headlights. No power out here, just phone lines. These people had kerosene for everything, or they just didn't have it, and he admired them for it. Mrs. Coover and her sister lived in the musty past—real antique furniture, a wind-up Victrola, hundreds of books, moth-eaten animal trophies all along the walls. Whoever had been the sportsman of the family was long gone; they did have one man living with them, a nephew who was too weak to carry firewood. Larry had seen him in the store during the summer. He could barely handle a loaf of bread. He wore sunglasses and black gloves and carried an ivory-handled gun in a holster. One time the firemen all got him drunk at the Balsam and the guy claimed to be a war hero, got up on a table and nearly fell off. They still talked about it down at the firehouse, did funny imitations.

Whatever their peculiarities, the Coovers were a family, more so than the Beckers. Larry thought about dying and leaving his father and sister behind—definitely not a family, more like a sad statistic. Because of this inevitable consequence, he took precautions to stay alive.

The rain now came down and froze on everything, but he was almost done with Coover's. When he worked on these old places, to stay awake he would think about the strange people who owned them. He'd review all their bizarre behavior, their crazy demands. Put that up. Take it down, no put it up again. Do you want us to pay you now, or . . . No, you can pay me in ten years—my pockets are stuffed with money right now. He'd never said that to anybody, but he'd thought it plenty.

After a while, a snowmobile barrelled down the road toward the Point. Some fool at the wheel—you'd have to be a fool to take a machine out on the lake on a night like this. More than once Larry had wrapped chains around a half-sunken machine and pulled the darn thing out of the ice, and if Larry was lucky, whoever the fool was would treat him to a beer afterward. "It's on me, Larry. I owe it to you." "Okay. Sounds about even—I saved your two-thousand dollar snow machine; you bought me a beer."

He got in his truck and followed the tracks of the snow machine, until he was only a hundred yards from the Poplar Point boathouse. The snow machine was sitting out on the lake ice, just twenty yards beyond the boathouse, its headlight on. The driver was rocking it back and forth, sending out blue smoke, digging a hole.

Larry looked at his gas can in the back of the truck, but he wasn't thinking about lending it to the man when his snowmobile ran out of gas.

The man's voice called to him, "Is that you, Larry?"

He didn't answer, though he knew who had called. "Dig a nice big hole for yourself," Larry said softly. Then he looked at the decrepit boathouse. One more year and it would collapse into the lake anyway. Who do you think they'll blame?

"C'mon Larry, I need your help out here for a minute. Larry, I know it's you up there . . ."

Mickey ran upstairs from the bar. In her living room, she turned off the TV that was still going although both kids had gone to bed. She listened for the specifics coming over the Plectron hanging on the kitchen wall. She had Harold Shink and three other fire volunteers down in the bar who would need directions.

On the Plectron, old Johnny Shink was growling, "We have a boathouse here. We have a boathouse on Poplar Point. Fully involved. We have a fire at the old boathouse on Poplar Point, Hamilton Lake."

And then other voices came on from other stations, maybe Larry's voice. Probably not; he wasn't a talker. She ran down to the bar and told the guys what she had heard, then ran up to the third floor, where the dormer gave her a view over the trees toward the Point. It was Tommy's bedroom. He woke up and moaned.

"Mom, what're you doing? Is it time for school?"

"No, honey," she said in a high pitch, unable to cover her fear. "I'm just looking at something over by the lake."

"A fire, right?"

The flames lit up the entire bay and turned the water to gold. Trees stood in silhouette like broken rakes. You would think a rain like this would put the fire out. It made her wonder what or who was feeding the fire, but she stopped herself before she wondered too hard.

LOST RIVER

They lost sight of the frozen river, the arc that flashed a half mile below the ski trail when the woods thinned out, the smooth ice that caught five different shades of sunset in its elbow shape, turned medium gray blue, then disappeared entirely at the next lookout.

"Lost River," Phil mumbled, saying its name out of the same frustration as those who had named it a hundred years before. The people had no trail then, only the river to guide them. As they followed the river, it spiraled in towards some unwanted center, and so they gave up, walked away from it, and named it.

Lost River ultimately lent its name to the small settlement that grew up a few miles south of its most southern bend. And the river itself was forgotten, with no mention but the rusted white sign where the west branch of Lost River crossed the highway, hardly a trickle there. When people said "Lost River" now, they almost always meant the town, not the river. The defunct downhill ski area and the two empty motels, snow blowing in and out of the windows. The highway garage, the old school, the Lost River Inn where everybody went for a drink, the random trailers and cabins that stretched out five miles along highway 235. You couldn't tell which were lived in, which abandoned, until nighttime when the lamps shone out of small windows, and the snow turned lighter shades of blue and orange in odd shapes over the wood piles and tire piles that surrounded the places where people made their homes.

For all its desolation and poverty, the town of Lost River had a businessmen's association (mainly bar owners) who raised money each winter for charity and publicity by sponsoring a treasure hunt. The treasure hunters paid a five-dollar entry fee and went out on two trail loops—one for skiers and one for snowmobilers. Each group searched for a gold brick (an ordinary red brick painted gold), redeemable for free meals at the Lost River Inn and twenty gallons of gasoline at Earl Shink's Mobil and other modest prizes at local merchants. Prizes worth over a hundred dollars. The clues had been adding up over the past week, broadcast over the radio.

"Final clue for you skiers," the announcer had said that morning at eleven. " 'Bend an elbow by the bar.' I don't make 'em up folks. I just read 'em."

Phil Gross set out with his younger brother Tom on the north end of the cross-country skiers' loop, where it angled southwest into the Lost River wilderness. "We have five hours of daylight," Tom said. "Let's do it right." Phil laughed when he remembered last year's treasure hunt, when the skiers' brick finally turned up in the tank of a toilet in the men's room at the Coffee Shop, something about water conservation in the final clue; he couldn't remember the exact wording—"Waste not, want not." Jack Getter had found it. The big fuss came when the women thought they had been excluded from the prize, until the snowmobilers' brick turned up in the wastebasket of the ladies room right next door—"Hens" next to "Roosters." For that brick, the clue had been scatalogical. More complaints.

At four-thirty Tom and Phil turned on their headlamps. They were glad to be out skiing together. They'd missed it last winter when Tom was stationed in Germany.

The ski trail narrowed gradually from the trailhead, and was now contained in a four-foot-wide trench made even deeper on each side by the thick growth of white pine, part of a reforestation project from the Depression years. You couldn't leave this part of the trail even if your life depended on it; you could barely turn around. Phil sometimes thought he could ski without the headlamp, the tracks were so good. Dozens of people had already gone through earlier in the week—but no one else today, because only Tom and Phil had thought of the bend in the river, the one that was shaped like an elbow when you looked at it from the top of Spruce Mountain. They'd always called it The Elbow, the tip of it The Funnybone.

"They're all at the Lost River Inn getting drunk," Tom said. "Bending an elbow."

"Yeah, they took one look at 'bar' and couldn't think of any other meaning. They'll tear that place apart. Paul Chester and his dad, the worst of that bunch."

"Chuck Norland, I would have thought," Tom said.

"Didn't you hear? He's locked up in Dannemora."

"That's a relief. I wonder if we'll find our treasure pretty soon." They stood next to each other in the double tracks, and Tom stamped his skis. "Where'd our skis get wet anyway?" he asked.

"Mine are okay. I jumped back there, you didn't," Phil said.

"No, I think you broke the ice back there, fatso. You made the stream flow again."

Phil stopped to let Tom catch up. "Do you think it'll glow in the dark?"

"No, but I don't want to get in any deeper. These skis are like logs now." Tom propped up his left ski without taking it off and Phil's headlamp scanned the inch of ice that had formed on the bottom. "Just this one ski," Tom said. Phil got out his plastic scraper and chopped off as much ice from Tom's ski as he could.

"This kind of hard work fogs my glasses. Let's get going. You'll be okay now."

They turned right on a side trail that Phil knew from summer hiking, heading north towards the bend of the river through untracked snow on an old tote road. Phil kept it clear for this very purpose, but it was an unofficial trail, unmarked by yellow plastic disks, no sign to tell the uninitiated where it might lead. Phil knew it would go down to the edge of the river where he had camped and fished several years ago, on The Funnybone. They were out of the thick pines now, gliding through second-growth beech mostly, an open woods that offered an occasional glimpse of the river, still catching gray light from the west.

They stopped to rest, and Phil took two Almond Joys out of his fanny pack.

"This is the best kind of skiing, anyway," he told his brother. "We both needed to get out and do this." They worked in construction, but it had been slow that year, and they had put on weight sitting around the Inn with the other guys who weren't working. Their friends were all charging around on snow machines looking for the other gold brick that Phil had hidden under the Lost River bridge.

"You think they've found it yet? The snowmobilers?" Tom asked.

"The lazy bums!"

" 'Lost is found, highway bound.' That's pretty obscure."

"Yeah, except the other clues were really obvious about a bridge. You know, like 'Don't be late for the golden gate.' "

"They're already celebrating," Tom said, wadding up the candy wrapper and stuffing it inside his pocket. "Maybe I should tear this up and drop it every few yards as we go."

"What's wrong with you, soldier? Scared of something?"

"Hell no. Let's go." They both laughed.

They saw dog tracks for a while. "Coydogs," Phil said.

A north wind kicked up and blew the fine powdered snow through the hemlocks. Phil had to tamp down the trail where it had drifted over. Tom waited behind Phil and slid his skis back and forth while he waited, afraid the ice would build up again if he stayed in one place too long and warmed the snow under his feet.

"What time's it getting to be? How much longer do we have?"

"It's over when it's over," Phil said.

A few yards from the edge of Lost River, they both had to fall down to stop. It was what Tom called a "controlled crash." Although the air temperature was below zero, the water remained open along the Funnybone, fed by warm springs.

"I don't think this is it," Phil said.

"You gotta be kidding."

"I smell smoke. Where the hell are we?"

"You tell me."

"This way."

After five minutes of following the edge of the river, Phil lost confidence in his sense of direction. But the smell of smoke became stronger and he heard a distant sound like a human voice or a coydog howling. Before long, they were skiing over fresh snowshoe tracks and forgetting why they had set out in the first place. He looked back over his shoulder and saw the crest of Hogback, the tiny spruce trees encrusted with snow, lit up on the east horizon. The old fire tower looked like a faint star.

Tom filled his head with a song he'd heard when driving into town listening to WRTY for treasure hunt clues. "Don't give me a hard time, woman, now that I've begged and pleaded, asked you for your love again." No, not those words, but words that rhymed and had a similar meaning. Maybe he had screwed up the clues. The words were supposed to rhyme, weren't they? Well, you couldn't write while driving. You'd go off the road and kill yourself trying to do that. "Bend an elbow by the bar. The golden treasure won't be far." That was it. Nothing particular in the second part.

Phil and Tom pulled up by a woodshed that looked like its roof would collapse if it snowed another inch. The snowshoe tracks went every which way, and the soft light from a cabin window, a hundred feet away, made a long golden trapezoid across the snow.

"God, who do you suppose lives here?"

"Take a look, Tommy." He aimed his headlamp at a crudely painted sign that had been nailed into a tree: PROPERTY OF EUGENE ROBERSON. INTRUDERS WILL BE SHOT.

"Nobody can own this. It's State land."

"You know how old he is?" Phil said. "Actually I always thought he was dead."

"I don't even know *who* he is."

"He's gotta be eighty, ninety. He was the ranger in the fire tower over at Hogback a long time ago. I guess he moved down here when they closed the tower."

"Buckskin?"

"The one and only."

"Ninety? I'd say a hundred."

"Hello? Hello?" Phil waited, thought he'd hear an echo. "He's out looking for his dog. I see dog tracks."

"He's stone deaf," Tom said. "He's a hundred, I tell ya."

"Maybe he's got a radio and we can find out who won."

"Looks just like the cabin he had on Hogback. When they tore it down maybe they gave him the boards." He saw the snowshoes hanging from a nail on the porch. "Not out on his snowshoes anyway," he whispered. They took off their skis and set them against the porch rail.

"Maybe he has two sets of snowshoes. There's no one in here now. Look, it's just one room." Phil pointed to the front window where they could see into the single room, with its barrel stove almost in the middle, the room full of smoke, only a faint wash of light from a kerosene lantern that sputtered on the side wall. A round map mounted on a board hung on the opposite wall, next to a crude bookcase made of stacked crates that went all the way to the ceiling.

"Hey I'm cold, Phil, let's go in."

The door pushed open easily but with a high shrieking noise. A thin dusting of snow lay on the floor, and they both looked at their dark bootprints. Phil gazed around as if he were still searching for

the gold brick. "Your glasses are completely fogged, you big jerk,"
Tom said.

"All right. What do you see?"

"Mouse turds. A mouse skeleton. A chamber pot, recently used.
An army cot, recently slept in. Soup cans. The old guy has a touch
of class—lace curtains. Holes in them."

Phil felt the map, and when his glasses defogged, he traced the
pattern of Lost River as it spiraled into nowhere.

"God!" Tom was looking out a head-sized hole in the lace curtain
of the back window, his headlamp still on, spotlighting the frozen
face of the dead man who lay in a bed of snow behind the cabin, the
wind blowing and polishing the man's icy features, his perfect
mustache.

They didn't go out behind the cabin. Better not to leave any
tracks near the old man's body. They kicked away their footprints,
strapped on their skis, and took off to the west, following the
snowshoe tracks. They no longer smelled smoke, but Phil thought
he smelled something else. "I know where we're headed now," he
yelled back at his brother.

"The sweat's frozen on my back."

"Sweat? I didn't think you sweated."

"I do when I'm scared," Tom said. "Where the hell are you going
now?"

"Snowmobile loop. Can't you smell the exhaust?"

"I can just smell your constant farts."

"Well, I'm scared too."

The river bent north there, and Tom looked at the polished ice.
The moon had come up and reflected on the ice, its outline diffused,
its shape elongated. "God, I've never seen anything like that before,"
he said. He meant the moon and the dead body, both sights. He
could hear the chainsaw-like whining of a distant snowmobile, and
the wind blowing through the hemlocks. The snow formed rippled
dunes against the east bank of the river.

"I sure hope it blows over our trail," Phil said. "Completely
covers it. Erases it."

"He's been dead for weeks maybe."

"Who lit the fire? Who lit the lantern?"

"The guy in these snowshoes," Tom said. "Suppose we'll track him down?"

Phil poked at a snow-encrusted hemlock with his ski pole.

"Nah," he finally said. "I'm just trying to find a way out of here before I get hypothermia and start hallucinating." A snowmobile barreled past only ten yards away from them, racing at fifty miles an hour, then another, bouncing over a blowndown tree that lay across the trail. Phil didn't know the trail, but he thought he'd go clockwise (southwest at first, then who knows?). Eventually they'd get back to the highway bridge where the other brick was hidden. He would check to see whether it was still there. Beyond that, he had no plans.

The new powder already covered the welts and gas stains the snowmobiles had laid down on the old snow. It was mostly uphill now, and Phil had to admit he was out of shape. His throat was salty, like he'd taken a swig of warm salt water. He spat once, then realized he could dehydrate if he kept that up, then thought he could chew snow, then thought of the cold lump that would form in his stomach. He remembered a short cut that would save them at least two miles getting back to the highway. The side trail switched back on a ridge with a lookout to the north. Phil and Tom stood there in their skis for a long time, gazing at the lightshow along the west bank of Lost River, a mile north of where they had left it, the snowmobiles buzzing along what looked like a shelf above the water, outlining the shore of the river that would have otherwise been invisible. All Phil could think of was shooting stars. There's a shooting star when anyone dies. Is that what this display meant? So much of what happened at Lost River (the town, not the river) lacked any intention at all; if any event seemed to have meaning, it was only a coincidence—though when he turned his lamp on his brother's face and saw what he thought was a tear frozen on his cheek, he believed there might be more than a coincidence in the meaning he read there.

The two of them had aimed their headlamps at the old man like spotlights, circling like inept predators. The light trembled as their heads trembled. "God," Tom had said over and over. "I remember him. God! What a place to die." Snow blew in and out of the old man's mouth like smoke. Phil remembered him, too. He remembered old Buckskin in the tower, who had represented his future, what he wanted to be—guardian of the woods, in a khaki uniform with a badge and a hat. Almost fifteen years ago, and Buckskin had been old then.

"You're not crying over him?" he asked his brother.

"What do you mean? I'm not crying. I *don't* cry. I'm just thinking. I'm trying to make it snow hard for the next few days. A foot would do it. Then a deep freeze. A little rain. Then another deep freeze to make a hard crust. Keep him cold there until the County Sheriff goes in there with his snow machine."

If it got warm enough they knew the coydogs would find him.

Roger Sheffer grew up in Saratoga County and camped and hiked in the Adirondacks during his childhood. He has his Doctor of Arts in English from SUNY Albany. In 1980, he moved out to Minnesota to take a teaching job at Mankato State University, but he has managed to come back to New York State every summer. Lately, he has retreated for a month to a camp near Canada Lake, where he writes and hikes and visits with his family.

His work has been published in *South Dakota Review, Nebraska Review, Mississippi Valley Review, Blueline,* and other publications.

Other Night Tree Press Titles

Yammering Away: The Best of "Letters Home"
Commentary on the North Country and Life in General
by Gregg Fedchak

"Letters Home" is Gregg Fedchak's weekly newspaper column which appears in the Park Newspapers of St. Lawrence, Inc. THE NEW YORK PRESS ASSOCIATION AWARDED "LETTERS HOME" FIRST PLACE IN THE FEATURE COLUMN CATEGORY FOR WEEKLY NEWSPAPERS OF ANY SIZE CIRCULATION IN 1986.

In *Yammering Away: The Best of "Letters Home,"* readers get to feel the true spirit of the North Country of New York State as vividly portrayed by an award-winning young essayist.

"Fedchak's stories are folksy and often funny and, while entertaining, instructive in the philosophy of life in the "slow lane."
   —Ken Pokalsky
    New York Alive

Library of Congress Catalog Number 85-91018
ISBN 0-935939-00-8 $9.95

The Way to Heron Mountain
poetry by Ed Zahniser
illustrations by Grace Oehser

The Way to Heron Mountain affirms the simple lifestyle that so many Adirondack and North Country people live. Ed Zahniser's poems make natives feel blessed, while all other readers are gently drawn Adirondack-ward.

"This is a soothing, loving book: a series of poems about a man who lives alone seeking wisdom in the Adirondacks. In it we find peace and grace."
   —Annie Dillard, author of the Pulitizer Prize-winning
    PILGRIM AT TINKER CREEK and six other books

Library of Congress Catalog Number 86-061605
ISBN 0-935-939-01-6 $3.95

To order, include check or money order for total price of books ordered, plus $1.50 for postage and handling. New York State residents please include 7% sales tax. Send your order to:
   NIGHT TREE PRESS
   R.D.#2, Box 140-G
   The Gorge Road Rt. 46
   Boonville, New York 13309